WHITE CHRISTMAS

A SHORT HOLIDAY ROMANCE

COME HOME FOR CHRISTMAS
BOOK TWO

SYLVIA MCDANIEL

An Unforgettable Blizzard of Love -- Second Chances With a Billionaire

In the heart of a raging snowstorm, fate reunites Emma Miller and billionaire Theodore White, two old high school friends. Emma, with no room left in the city and Theodore on his way to Whitefish, Montana, is forced to land at the Missoula airport.

Back in school, Emma was Theodore's steadfast protector, standing up to bullies on his behalf. Now, stranded on his private jet for three days, the forced proximity of their unexpected reunion sparks a passionate connection that defies reason, a love that had been simmering for years finally ignites.

In this enchanting tale of insta-love and second chances, they discover that the snowstorm that brought them together may just be the miracle needed to heal old wounds and spark a love that was always meant to be. Can they weather the storm and find love amidst the snowflakes, giving their past friendship a chance at a new, heartwarming future?

Coming Home for Christmas

I'll Be Home for Christmas
White Christmas
Santa's Baby
All I Want For Christmas
Box Set

Love books? Love deals? Love a little mischief? Sign up for my
Substack—it's free!
Click Here to join

CHAPTER 1

*E*mma Miller hated flying.

Actually, *despised* was a more accurate word. Hurtling through the sky in a metal tube with recycled air, luke-warm coffee, and zero legroom? Yeah, she could live a hundred years without it and be just fine.

But flying into small regional airports like *Missoula, Montana?* That was next-level torture. Especially in winter. Especially when connecting flights were few, the weather was unpre-dictable, and you had better odds of riding a reindeer to your final destination.

She crossed her legs in the plastic chair by the gate and stared at the growing storm through the floor-to-ceiling windows. Thick, dark clouds gathered above the mountains like a threat whispered by nature itself.

Not good.

The sign still flashed "Delayed," mocking her with its stubborn glow. But for how long? Another hour? All night? Dread coiled in her stomach, any longer and she'd be sleeping in this freezing terminal with nothing but a vending machine dinner and fluo-rescent lights buzzing overhead.

Already, she could see a line forming at the rental car counter. Her heart sank. Were they all about to be stranded here? Were they beating her to a car?

She pulled out her phone and tapped through the local weather updates.

Blizzard Warning in Effect

Whitefish expected to receive 5–6 feet of snow in the next 48 hours.

"What the hell am I even doing here?" she muttered to herself.

It wasn't like she looked forward to the family Christmas. Not anymore. Not with Olivia, who seemed to constantly be in crisis. Or Amelia, her practically perfect twin sister with her golden glow and unflappable charm.

Meanwhile, she was the "smart one." The "responsible one." The overachiever who paid her own rent, filed her taxes early, and quietly climbed the ladder at her company while no one really asked what ladder it was.

She could become the President of the United States, and her parents would probably ask if she was getting enough sleep.

So, what exactly do you do again, Emma?

She rolled her eyes at the memory, staring just in time to watch a sleek private jet land effortlessly on the runway. A Learjet. Of course. Probably someone flying in from Aspen or Vail for a weekend of skiing and cocoa served by staff in matching Patagonia jackets.

Must be nice.

Like a voice from the heavens, the announcement echoed through the terminal, not with salvation, but with the weight of a funeral dirge, heavy and foreboding.

"We regret to inform you that all flights out of Missoula have been canceled due to the incoming storm. Please check with a gate agent. Baggage will be returned to carousel three."

There it was. Her worst travel nightmare coming true.

Stranded.

She shot to her feet and immediately dialed hotels nearby,

cradling her phone between her shoulder and cheek while she opened her travel app.

"No availability."

"We're full, ma'am."

"You might try the Gilded Palace out by the truck stop."

Oh, hell no.

She'd driven past that place once. It looked like the set of a B-grade horror movie, or worse, a hotbed of bacteria and bad decisions.

With a groan, she plopped back into her seat. *Could she even sleep here at the airport?*

There was no way she was braving the Gilded Petri Dish.

Her eyes darted toward the rental car counter again. The line had thinned. Maybe there was still a shot.

Worth a try.

Snatching her purse, she practically jogged to the counter. "I'll take whatever car you've got. I don't care if it's a scooter with snow tires."

The woman behind the counter blinked, clearly exhausted from dealing with angry travelers. "We have a 2018 Toyota Camry. High mileage but solid."

"I'll take it—"

"I was here first."

A male voice spoke from just behind her, deep, smooth, and unmistakably annoyed. And familiar.

She stiffened. Could he not see her?

"I'm literally standing at the counter."

"Yeah, and I was walking up to it before you cut in line."

"I didn't cut. I claimed."

The man had been walking while texting. It wasn't her problem, he had moved too slow.

The clerk held up her hands. "Too late. Just rented it to a seventy-year-old woman who looked like she could throw down. I'm out of cars."

Emma groaned. *Perfect.* No hotel. No flight. No rental car. This was shaping up to be the most festive holiday ever.

And then she heard it. That voice again.

Softened this time. Almost… surprised.

"Emma?"

She turned.

And the moment stretched.

Emerald green eyes blinked at her. A face she hadn't seen in more than a decade, but one she recognized immediately.

Holy. Hell.

Theo White.

Her brain stuttered. *Theodore White.* The kid who used to sit two rows behind her in AP Calculus. The quiet genius who created a video game during lunch period. The boy with thick glasses, no fashion sense, and the social skills of a bookshelf.

Except… that boy was long gone. And this man had all her erogenous zones firing on high alert. What the hell was he doing in the airport in Missoula?

CHAPTER 2

*E*mma Miller, his high school crush, stood at the rental-car desk, framed by the harsh airport lights, and he nearly stopped breathing. The girl he'd loved from afar in high school, the quiet one, the brilliant one, the one who protected him from bullies, was here, in real life, and more beautiful than his memory dared allow. Light auburn hair haloed her face; eyes that used to shyly avoid his now stared back at him with surprise, strength, and something tender.

He swallowed and drew a steadying breath, forcing himself forward. The years in between might have been heavy, but he would not show the cracks now.

"Emma," he said gently, letting his voice carry what his heart did not.

Her head whipped in his direction. Surprise flooded her features. Her mouth parted, eyes alight with shock and maybe something faint like longing.

"Theo? Is that really… you?" she whispered, as though hearing his name in her own mind had woken a dream.

"It's me," he said, forcing a slight, uncertain grin. "Wow. It's been too long."

She nodded, tipping her chin with disbelief. "You look… different. Stronger." Her tone was soft, mingled with marvel.

That moment, stuttering, breathtaking, was everything he'd waited for. He remembered her at seventeen, standing up for him when he had no voice, her kindness a shield. The world had changed them, but the core of her remained.

"How are you?"

"Stuck here at the airport, just like you," she said.

He cleared his throat. "Missoula grounded us. The wind's too dangerous ahead. My pilot refused to push us farther."

She exhaled sharply, frustration folding her shoulders inward. "Great. Just what I needed—weather to ruin Christmas."

Behind them, counters flicked to "Out of Service," agents posted "No Cars Available" signs. The terminal hummed with tension. Travelers clustered in corners, phones glued to ears, faces drawn.

He offered what little calm he had. "Want to share a taxi to a hotel? Or at least a coffee while the options diminish?"

She shook her head. "They're all full. I tried. Nothing left."

His chest constricted. This wasn't good. The storm wasn't just incoming, it was a predator. She was trapped with him now. And he didn't want to be just a companion. He wanted to be the one she leaned on.

He nodded. "Okay." Then, gesturing: "Café?"

She accepted with a tired but brave smile. They drifted toward the small food counter, sandwiched between airline counters. They grabbed lukewarm coffee and stale wraps, watching the clerk's face grow paler as the crowd swelled behind them.

He watched her delicately sip coffee, her fingers warmed by the cup. He wondered how many nights she'd been like this, alone, wondering if her own life would ever feel steady. He wondered how many times she'd put her dreams in second place.

At least the girl he knew in high school had always looked

after everyone else. Especially, her sisters. Their needs came before her own and he hoped she no longer looked after them.

They sat across from one another. He suppressed the urge to reach over and touch her hair. To grab her hand, to just feel her satiny skin once again.

She looked at him with curious tenderness. "You're doing well, Theo. I followed your company's growth after college."

He exhaled quietly, gratitude and vulnerability mingling. "White Gaming Systems. My father and I started it. We craft educational games, simulation modules... things people don't always realize teach them. I wanted to build something that gives power to others—kids, teens, anyone who felt ignored."

Her eyes widened, and she nodded. "I always knew you had that in you."

He felt his heart both warm and ache. Her belief in him felt more like acceptance than any boardroom contract ever had. More precious.

He turned the question to her: "What about you, Emma? What are you doing now?"

She swallowed, an edge of weariness mixing with pride. "NICU nurse. I care for tiny lives when hope is stretched thin. And I started PA school. I want to do more. To be more present."

He nodded, impressed. That calling took courage.

"You're not married?" he asked softly.

"No, I'm too busy working and going to school," she said. "I hope to graduate next summer. After that, I don't know what I'll be doing," she said. "How about you? I'd think you would be married by now."

Shaking his head, he sighed. He'd come close once, but then learned she was not in love with him but rather his bank account.

"No wife, no girlfriend," he said. "Women still think I'm a nerd."

Or even worse, they only dated him because they knew he

had money. He'd yet to find someone who wanted him. And that was what he was searching for. Someone like Emma.

She shook her head, laced her fingers. "I didn't meet someone I couldn't live without. And I won't settle. My parents taught me what love *should* be. I'm still waiting for someone who looks at me the way I look at them."

His chest tortured him. He wanted to be the someone who looked at her that way.

Emma laughed, and the sound sent a trickle of pure awareness racing through him. Staring at her full lips, he couldn't help but wonder how she would taste. She'd been his crush, and yet he'd never pursued her in high school because he didn't think she would want to go out with a boy like him.

They'd been the best of friends and hung out all the time together, studying, playing games, and talking trash about the jocks in school.

She was the quieter, the more introverted of the Miller twins. Her sister had been the most popular girl in school and he'd never thought he would have a chance with Emma.

"How's Amelia," he asked.

Shaking her head, she frowned. "She's still the same. Last I spoke to her she was dating a congressman's son. She's an attorney working for a big firm in Cheyenne, Wyoming. We don't speak often because all I hear about is how wonderful her life is and everything is going her way."

"Not the same for you?" he asked.

"My life is good, but I deal with babies on the edge of death. Some we save, some we have to let go. And it shows you how precious life is. And then going to school at the same time, it takes a lot out of you."

He could understand that. Sometimes he considered going back for his doctorate, but then why? The business was successful and he was creating new games and he had a focus group of teenagers that tested them for him.

At that moment, a fight broke out near the refrigerator, two men arguing viciously over the few remaining sandwiches. "I saw them first!"

"My kids need them!"

The commotion escalated until security intervened and parceled out the food.

Emma winced. "That's… bleak."

He placed his hand over hers, solace in contact. "In times like this, even kindness is scarce."

She nodded, then looked at him resolutely, green eyes flickering. The world outside threatened. Inside, something new flickered.

"Are you on your way to Whitefish?"

"Yes," he said. "My parents are expecting me. What about you?"

"Yes," she replied. "We're all gathering for Christmas for the first time in several years. My mother wanted us all to come home this year."

He took a breath, weighed his words, and then said, "Hey, my private jet is sitting out on the tarmac. Would you like to see it?"

For a moment, she seemed unsure, and then she smiled. "Why not? I'm not going anywhere."

None of them were, and it looked like things could get tense here in the terminal. Maybe he could convince her to stay on his jet with him. It would give them time together. Time to see if his fantasies could come true.

CHAPTER 3

The man was smoking hot.

When Theo reached for her hand, Emma didn't expect to feel anything beyond polite gratitude. But the moment his fingers wrapped around hers, firm, warm, possessive in a way that made her heart stumble, something shifted.

A current of heat curled down her spine, subtle and slow, like the very beginning of a flame.

He led her through the glass security doors and into the cold. Snow had begun to fall softly, fat flakes dancing under the yellow glow of the floodlights on the tarmac. The world was quiet, too quiet, and the silence pressed against her skin like a whisper she couldn't quite catch.

Above them, the sky was black velvet, thick with storm. She'd never seen anything like it. The snow wasn't just falling. It was creeping, closing in, swallowing the horizon one lazy inch at a time.

This wasn't just weather. It was a warning.

Her boots crunched across the icy pavement as she followed Theo toward the jet. His jet. It didn't hit her until they rounded the corner of the building and saw it fully parked in the snowlit darkness: the sleek, silver Boeing Business Jet she'd seen land earlier.

She stopped walking, momentarily stunned.

Oh my God.

The plane was massive. Not just "nice" or "private," but *opulent*. Powerful. A beast with wings. The kind of thing CEOs flew in spy movies, or kings used to cross oceans. She suddenly felt small beside it. Small and unprepared for all the ways Theo White had changed since high school.

Not just his body, though yes, *dear Lord*, that transformation was criminal, but everything about him. His presence. His quiet confidence. His command of space.

Theo radiated a quiet, magnetic authority—no trace of the squeaky, uncertain boy from high school, but a man fully in command, his presence filling the space like heat.

She watched him walk up to the stairs like he belonged here. And he did. This wasn't some rental or shared charter. This was his. And yet…

The part that twisted inside her wasn't envy.

It was awe. Admiration. The tiniest flicker of possibility. She wasn't just following him into a plane. She was stepping into a world she hadn't expected, one she didn't know if she belonged in, but wanted to understand.

"I think the storm's arrived," he said as they reached the stairs, wind snatching at his words.

She nodded, her voice lost to the gusts. *Yes.* And she wasn't just talking about the weather.

The metal steps were slick underfoot, but he held her suitcase and offered his hand again as she climbed. The moment their palms touched, the flutter came back, stronger this time, deeper, lower.

The door opened with a hiss, revealing a woman in a crisp navy pantsuit and an immaculate chignon. "Welcome aboard," she said with a smile.

Emma stepped inside and was immediately wrapped in warmth, heat, light, quiet opulence.

"Jenny, this is Emma," Theo said beside her, his voice low and firm.

The stewardess smiled again. "It's a pleasure to have you on board."

Emma gave a small nod, unsure of how to respond. Was she his guest? A friend? Something more? She didn't know, and somehow, the not-knowing made her feel... alive.

A man appeared from a side hallway, tall, weathered, in a pilot's jacket. "Sir, we're socked in. No chance of takeoff tonight, maybe not even tomorrow. This storm's a monster."

"Thanks, Frank. Emma, this is my pilot, Frank."

"Hi," she said, her voice more breath than word.

"Nice to meet you," he replied, then stepped aside.

Theo placed a gentle hand on her lower back, not intrusive, just... present. Anchoring. "Come on, I'll give you the tour."

They moved past the galley, sleek steel appliances, a fridge bigger than the one in her apartment, shelves full of snacks and drinks, then into a conference room with a glass table and six leather chairs.

"I work here a lot when I fly," Theo said. "Game design doesn't really take time off."

She smiled at that. "Still a workaholic?"

"Maybe," he said, giving her a sideways glance that made her stomach do a quiet backflip. "But I don't hate what I do."

They walked past a narrow hallway to what he called the "quiet room"—a lounge with sofas, windows, and a giant screen on the wall. Cozy, but impressive.

And then he opened the last door.

"This is the master," he said, stepping aside to let her see.

It was... stunning. A king-size bed. Dim lighting that felt like dusk. Soft cream walls. Real bedding. A shower visible through a half-open door, tiled in black marble. This wasn't a plane. It was a luxury apartment with wings.

Her throat tightened. "Wow," she whispered. "Theo… you could live here."

He chuckled. "I have, during launches. Or when I just need to disappear for a while."

Disappear.

She knew that word too well.

They stood in the doorway, inches apart. She glanced up and found him looking at her, not with arrogance or even expectation, but something gentler. Curious. Intent.

"I can't imagine flying like this," she said.

"Most people never do. It's not normal. It's a perk. And a reminder of how crazy this journey has been."

She looked away. "You've done well."

His voice was soft. "You helped me survive it. Back then. You were… kind. That matters more than you think."

She didn't know what to say. Praise from him now, *this* version of Theo, felt so different. It didn't roll off her back. It landed.

"Let's sit," he said, and led her back to the lounge. A platter of snacks had been set out: nuts, crackers, fruit, and bottled water. He poured her a glass without asking.

He'd never been a big drinker in high school, even when Amelia and her friends had invited them to partake in the spiked punch at a party. He never smoked. They had been the Goody-Two-Shoes at school, and it never bothered her. After working at the hospital, she'd quickly realized she was so glad she'd never been involved with drugs or alcohol.

A shift in the ER had quickly made her realize the dangers.

She took it, fingers brushing his. Another pulse of heat rushed through her veins.

Stop it, she told herself. *This is Theo.*

But that was the problem, wasn't it?

This wasn't the old Theo. Not the skinny kid she used to help with science projects. Not the quiet boy who never fought back when the jocks messed with his locker. This was a man, tall, sculpted, self-assured, and entirely too handsome for her to ignore.

And she didn't *want* to ignore him.

"What have you heard about anyone from our class?"

"Not much," she said. "Several of the girls got married right after we graduated. James Clark went into the military and was killed overseas. Billy Smith graduated from college and then attended medical school. What have you heard?"

These people were more her sister's friends than hers. Frankly, once she'd left, she wanted to put high school behind her. Those days were over. College had been easier, and the friends she made there, she still kept in touch with.

"Remember how Larry Martin use to give me so much crap and grief in school?"

"Yes," she said, her brows drawing together. "He was so mean."

She'd gotten so mad at the asshat for the way he treated Theo. She'd even threatened to expose that he cheated on his exams to continue playing football if he didn't leave Theo alone. For months, she'd watched as he harassed poor Theo for being so smart while Larry was dumber than a box of rocks.

"You're not going to believe this. When he learned that I was doing so well, he came to me and asked me to loan him some money," he said shaking his head.

Stunned, she stared at him. "What did you do?"

"Well, you remember he was always stealing my lunch?"

"Yes," she said. "How many times did he either take your food or dump your tray?"

"Too many to count," he said.

"What did you do?"

"I told him I would loan him the money, but that not only would he have to pay me back with twelve percent interest, but he would have to pay off every child's overdue lunch account at Spartan Elementary, Griffin Middle School, and Whitefish High School."

Laughter bubbled up from her chest. That was brilliant.

"Did he take the offer?"

"No," he said. "Since that day, I've not heard from or seen him."

She laughed again, her body relaxing, warming. She hadn't laughed like this in months. Maybe years.

A sharp gust hit the side of the plane. The cabin creaked slightly. Snow had begun to fall in thick waves. The windows were nearly white. Even the terminal lights were gone now—swallowed by wind and cold.

She shivered, and not entirely from the chill.

"You should stay here tonight," he said. "You'll be safer. And more comfortable."

He said it so matter-of-factly, without pressure or hint, that it took her a moment to process it. Her heart skipped.

"I'll stay for a bit," she said cautiously. "Not committing to anything."

His smile deepened. "Just like high school. You were always the cautious one."

"And you were always the sweet one."

He leaned forward slightly, elbows resting on his knees, his gaze sharp now. Focused.

"You really think that's who I was? Sweet?"

"Yes," she said, surprised at the sudden tightness in her chest. "You didn't try to be cool. Or mean. You just were... *you*. That meant something."

His voice dropped. "It still does."

The silence between them stretched. The plane swayed gently again. Outside, the world was a blur of snow and wind and night.

Inside, her heart beat too loud.

He reached for a throw blanket and handed it to her. Their fingers brushed again, slower this time. Lingering.

She watched his face, searching for the boy she used to know. He was still in there—under the sculpted jaw and quiet power. That beautiful nerd still lived in the corners of his smile.

And suddenly, she wanted to know *everything* about him. Not just the man he'd become—but the man he *was* now.

A smile spread across his face. "It will be fun," he said.

Another blast of wind hit the plane, and they glanced out the window. It was blowing snow so hard that she couldn't see the terminal. Even the lights had disappeared.

"I might not have any choice," she said.

"Maybe not," he replied. "I'm all right with that. I'll enjoy spending time with you just like old times."

Warmth filled her at the thought. But this time, that warmth came from her center, and she'd never felt that for Theo.

Her pulse spiked. She wrapped the blanket tighter around herself, both for comfort and because she wasn't sure what would happen if she didn't.

This was going to be one long, snowy night.

CHAPTER 4

Theo watched Emma lean toward the laptop screen in the faint, amber glow of the jet's cabin. Her profile—those rounded cheeks, that determined mouth, the faint crease between her brows—was a pull in his chest he could never seem to escape. Outside, the wind battered the fuselage, the storm a living thing pressing against steel and glass. Inside, though, the silence felt intimate. Almost sacred.

"I want to see what everyone's doing now," he said quietly. "Our class. Where life has taken them."

She nodded, curiosity softening her features, and moved closer. Their shoulders brushed, just enough to make his pulse stutter. They searched together—names, photos, marriages, kids, a few scattered obituaries. The ghosts of high school rearranged themselves into adult versions of the same faces that once filled his nightmares.

He recognized so many of them—the kids who'd mocked him, the jocks who'd shoved him into lockers, the girls who'd pretended not to know his name. And now? Half of them were small-town insurance agents or real estate brokers. Others posted selfies from dull office cubicles.

And then there was him—Theo White. Founder of **White Gaming Systems**, innovator, builder of digital worlds that millions of kids lived inside.

A quiet satisfaction stirred in his chest. *We built something better than they ever imagined.*

Maybe that was petty. But the cruelty of those years had been real. They hadn't just bruised his ego—they'd shaped him. Every insult, every lonely lunch, every whispered laugh behind his back had fueled the empire he'd built. It had forged him.

He felt Emma watching him. Her lips parted slightly, her eyes filled with warmth rather than pity. That was what undid him—she'd never pitied him, even back then.

She always saw me.

He remembered her in flashes: defending him on the steps outside the gym, glaring down the quarterback who'd called him "Four-Eyes," sliding her lunch apple onto his tray when the cafeteria ran out. She'd been his armor before he knew what armor was.

He turned to her. "That game—the one where the player stands up to the bully and saves the kid in trouble—that was mine."

Her breath caught. "The one I told you was brilliant?"

He smiled. "That's the one. When it went viral, millions of kids played it. They thought they were saving someone else, but really, it was me they were saving." His voice softened. "That game was built on kindness because of *you*, Emma."

She looked down, a shy, quiet pride flickering through her expression. He could almost see her processing it—what it meant to have inspired a world that taught courage.

Jenny entered then, gliding in with professional precision. "Cocktail hour," she announced. "What can I get you?"

"Do we still have champagne on board?" he asked, his voice rougher than intended.

"Yes, sir."

He straightened, the moment feeling bigger than a drink. "Bring us the bottle."

As Jenny disappeared, Theo caught Emma's gaze again—half amusement, half disbelief.

"Champagne?" she said with a smile.

He nodded. "To us. To rediscovering what got lost somewhere along the way. It's… good to see you, Emma. I've missed how you always made me laugh."

Her smile grew, soft and unguarded. In high school, she'd been pretty in that effortlessly natural way. Now, she was breathtaking. And not just because she'd grown into her beauty—she carried herself differently. Graceful. Steady. The kind of woman who didn't need to prove anything anymore.

When Jenny returned with the champagne, Theo poured them each a glass and raised his flute. "To finding each other again—and to being stranded together."

Emma laughed as their glasses touched. "To being stranded," she said. "Could've been worse company."

He smiled. "Much worse."

They sipped. He watched the way her lips brushed the rim of the glass, the way her throat moved as she swallowed. Every tiny gesture wrecked his composure.

"Want to play something?" he asked, reaching for the deck of cards near the console. "We used to play rummy for hours."

She tilted her head, amused. "We were kids, Theo."

He gave a slow grin. "Then call this nostalgia—with better champagne."

She laughed, and it filled the quiet space with something warm. "All right. One game."

He dealt the cards while outside, the storm hammered the wings. They played like old friends—easy banter, teasing remarks, shared memories between hands. But beneath it all was a new rhythm, a current neither could quite ignore.

The laughter came easy, but the silences that followed were

charged. She was right there, close enough to touch. Close enough to smell the faint citrus scent of her hair.

He caught himself studying her fingers—slender, steady, graceful as she arranged her cards—and the memory of those same hands passing him notes in algebra class hit him like a punch.

Don't fall too fast, he warned himself. *You already did once.*

Lightning flashed, followed by a low rumble. Emma startled slightly, and instinctively he reached over, his hand brushing hers. "Hey," he said softly. "It's all right. We're safe in here."

Her eyes met his, wide and luminous. "I know. It's just… the sound."

He didn't move his hand. Neither did she.

Jenny returned briefly with a tray of vegetables and dip. "Would you like me to fix dinner?"

Theo looked to Emma. "Hungry?"

"Not really," she said, her voice quiet.

He turned back to Jenny. "Then why don't you leave the bottle, and you're free for the night."

Jenny smiled. "Thank you, sir."

As she left, Theo caught the faint flicker of uncertainty in Emma's eyes—the unspoken question about who Jenny really was. He leaned forward. "She's just my assistant," he said gently. "Keeps me organized, makes sure I don't live on energy drinks and takeout. That's all."

Emma smiled, a little sheepish. "You've gotten used to being spoiled."

He chuckled. "Maybe. But I'd rather be the one doing the spoiling."

Her cheeks pinked, and for a moment, the air thickened between them.

He leaned back, studying her face. "You happy, Emma? With your life?"

She blinked at the question. "I am. Mostly. I love my work. I help babies fight to live. It's just… sometimes I wonder what I'm missing."

He nodded slowly, his chest tightening. "Same here."

She looked at him with something like understanding. "You have everything, Theo. Success. Money. Freedom."

He smiled faintly. "Everything except what matters most. Someone to come home to. Someone who actually sees me."

Her eyes softened. "That's the important part, isn't it? Finding the right person."

He nodded. "Yeah. And when you do, you hold on."

The quiet between them stretched—comfortable, warm, dangerous.

Emma took another sip of champagne and laughed lightly. "I've dated my fair share of losers."

"Worse than Harry Black?" he asked, grinning.

She nearly spat out her drink, laughing. "Oh, I'd completely forgotten about him. He tried so hard, bless him. I think I scared him off."

He grinned, dealing the next hand. "He was terrified of you."

"I wasn't exactly intimidating."

"You didn't have to be," he said softly. "You were you."

For a moment, the room fell still again. Outside, the storm howled. Inside, the air vibrated with something neither of them dared name.

Finally, she cleared her throat. "So what's the bet this time?"

He hesitated, then smiled. "If I win, you spend the night here —your own room, your own bed. If you win, I'll let you beat me at rummy for life."

Her lips curved. "Deal."

Thirty minutes later, he laid down his hand. "And that's game."

Her eyes narrowed in mock irritation. "You cheated."

"Never," he said. "But I'll accept my prize—your company for the night."

She laughed, shaking her head. "Fine. What are we playing for next?"

Theo leaned back, emboldened by champagne and proximity. "Clothing."

Her brows lifted. "Clothing?"

"Loser removes one item. The person who loses the most has to post a picture of us on our high school Facebook page."

She laughed—a melodic, husky sound that made his heart trip. "With our clothes on, I assume?"

"Unfortunately, yes." He grinned. "Let's take one now, before either of us loses too badly."

She leaned in close, her body pressed lightly against his as they made goofy faces for the camera. When he snapped the photo, he knew he'd keep it forever—not for nostalgia, but as proof that sometimes life gave you second chances.

When they straightened, she was still close—close enough for him to feel the heat radiating from her skin. Close enough to make him forget the snowstorm raging outside.

"Emma," he said quietly. "I'm glad I ran into you… even if you tried to steal my rental car."

She laughed softly. "I think we're better off here than stuck on some icy road."

He nodded. "Agreed."

She picked up her cards again. "You won the last one. I'm taking this round."

He smiled, slow and dangerous. "Who says I play fair?"

Her eyes gleamed. "You never did."

Their laughter mingled with the wind outside as another hand began—cards on the table, champagne on their tongues, and a storm brewing between them far more dangerous than anything beyond the glass.

And in that moment, Theo knew: this wasn't just a game anymore. It was the beginning of something real.

Something worth risking everything for.

CHAPTER 5

*E*mma didn't normally drink, but tonight felt like an exception to every rule she lived by. She was warm, a little light-headed, and far too aware of Theo sitting across from her, shirtless, grinning like a man who knew exactly how desirable he'd become.

She laughed, too loud maybe, but genuine. This was fun. It had been *so long* since something felt like fun.

She hadn't expected to feel so… herself with him again. Not guarded, not performing. Just *Emma*. It amazed her how easily their old rhythm had returned, as if a decade hadn't passed. And yet, it wasn't quite the same. The dynamic had shifted. Now, she noticed things about Theo that she had never dared to notice back then.

The width of his chest. The way the light carved shadows down his abs. The slight scruff along his jaw. And God help her, his eyes, brilliant, focused, always searching hers like she was a puzzle he couldn't stop solving.

Where the boy had once been sweet and brilliant and awkward, the man was devastating. And he still had that ridiculous brain behind all those biceps.

She'd forgotten how much fun she and Theo used to have together. She'd forgotten he'd been her best friend in school, and they had done everything as a team, not like a couple, but just as the best of friends. Their friendship had picked up right where they left off, and yet, this time, she was noticing things about him she'd never thought before.

"By the way," she said, swirling her champagne lazily, "how was Yale?"

He gave a crooked smile. "Filled with rich, entitled snobs." Then he shrugged. "But I graduated with honors while building my company, so I can't complain. It worked out."

Of course it had. She'd always known he would make something of himself. Still, a sliver of guilt slid under her skin. He should have been valedictorian. But Amelia had taken the title by a single point. One measly point. And Emma knew, she *knew*, that point had more to do with teacher bias than merit.

She sipped her drink and shook her head. "I always thought you deserved to be number one."

He looked at her then, not dismissing the sentiment, not brushing it away. "Thanks. That means more than you know."

"I mean it." Her voice caught slightly. "You've always had this focus, this spark. It's rare."

Theo smiled, but there was a quiet heaviness in it.

"You need to help me with my studies," she said, suddenly craving a lighter topic. "I'm drowning in coursework. I love it, but sometimes I think my brain's going to melt."

"You were going to med school, right? What changed?"

She shrugged, pulling her knees up onto the seat and hugging them lightly. "I thought so. But nursing felt more natural. And now, becoming a PA... I think I'll have the best of both worlds."

There was more to it than that, of course. A quiet craving to be done with school. To stop putting her life on hold. She wanted to live. She wanted more than textbooks and night shifts. She wanted love. A home. *Someone* to build something with.

He laid down his hand. "Rummy."

"Damn!" she said, laughing. "That was fast."

"Time to pay up," he said, voice dropping low, eyes dark with something unmistakable. "Remove a piece of clothing."

Heat curled through her belly.

She kicked off her boots, grinning. "There."

Theo laughed, head tilting. "Sneaky. You always were the conniving one."

"You love it," she teased, reshuffling the cards.

"Did you have a girlfriend in college?" she asked.

He paused. "Yeah. A few. Even got engaged once."

Her eyebrows shot up. "What? Theo White almost tied the knot?"

"She said yes," he said, shrugging. "And then I found out she loved my bank account more than me."

"Oof." She winced. "I'm sorry."

"It's fine. At least I found out before the wedding. Now I just… I don't know. I keep wondering if people are interested in me, or what I can *give* them."

Emma's heart clenched. She understood that, in her own way. She'd seen doctors charm nurses like trophies. She'd been flirted with, propositioned, dismissed, all without ever being truly *seen*.

"I get it," she said. "You want someone who makes your heart spin. Not someone who's keeping score."

"Exactly."

She laid down her hand. "Rummy."

His groan was theatrical. "You kicked my ass."

"Damn right I did. Take off your shirt."

He rose from the table with a sly grin and peeled the shirt over his head.

Emma's breath caught.

Holy hell.

The lean, lanky boy from her past had become a sculpted,

muscled Adonis. His chest rippled with definition, his abs a clear six-pack, arms taut and strong. She stared openly.

"I work with a trainer," he said casually. "Helps me keep sane."

"You've… changed," she whispered. "You're hot, Theo."

He rubbed the back of his neck, suddenly bashful. "Thanks. You're not so bad yourself."

She laughed. "Not so bad? I was fishing for stunning."

"Stunning. Absolutely."

Their eyes held. Something shifted. That subtle flirtation took on heat.

"Why are you hanging out with me?" she asked softly. "You look like a billionaire tech god. You could be anywhere. With anyone."

His voice dropped. "Because there's nowhere else I'd rather be."

Oh. Her stomach flipped.

"You're still you," she said quietly. "That's what I was worried about. That success would change you."

"It changed a lot," he admitted. "But not the part of me that remembers how you always stood up for me."

She smiled, a little ache blooming in her chest.

The next hand started. Their banter resumed. It was warm and easy and *so much more charged* than it had ever been before.

After a few minutes, he laid down his cards. "Rummy."

She groaned. "I was so close!"

He leaned in, eyes sparking. "Take off your shirt."

She laughed. "Or… I could take off my socks?"

"Nope. Shirt. Fair's fair."

The plane rocked gently as wind gusted against the fuselage.

Emma hesitated. "What if someone walks in?"

"They won't. I promise. Need more champagne?"

"Yes," she said, too quickly.

While he went to the galley, she slipped off her shirt and

grabbed his from the floor. She slid it on—soft, warm, and smelling like him.

When he returned, he stopped in the doorway.

"That's cheating," he said, eyes roaming her body.

"It's not cheating. My shirt's off. You never specified *which* shirt."

He poured her another glass and handed it over, his fingers brushing hers.

They clinked glasses again.

"To me, winning this next hand," she teased.

"Nope. Me. And then you're losing those jeans."

A thrill shot through her at his words. This was bold. Flirtatious. Dangerous. And she was loving every second of it.

It had been so long since she felt this alive.

She dealt the cards, and they both played quickly, the tension curling tighter with every draw. He laid down his hand again with that damn victorious smirk.

"Take them off."

"I could take off my other sock," she said.

He gave her a look. "Don't push it."

She stood slowly. Her hands trembled slightly, not from fear, but anticipation. "Maybe… maybe you should remove them."

He was on his feet in seconds. Heat radiated from his body as he approached.

His fingers touched the button of her jeans, and her breath hitched. She didn't stop him.

With practiced slowness, he unhooked them, sliding the zipper down.

Then he knelt.

His hands skimmed down her legs, dragging the jeans with them. Her breath came shallow, heart hammering.

"Damn, Emma," he whispered. "You're…"

His hands lingered as he helped her step out of them. He rose slowly, his palms trailing along her bare thighs, then hips.

She nearly whimpered.

Her hands went to his shoulders for balance. Instead, she found herself clutching him.

"Theo," she breathed.

His eyes met hers, dark, hungry. "I've wanted to do this for years."

And then his mouth was on hers.

His lips were warm and firm and searching. She melted into him, her hands sliding up his back, feeling the strength there. His tongue coaxed her open, and she kissed him like she'd wanted this all along. Like her body had always known it would come to this.

He groaned into her mouth. She gasped into his.

This wasn't a crush anymore.

This was the match being struck. Fire. Flame. Hunger.

She wasn't drunk. Maybe a little tipsy, but she was *clear*. She wanted him.

God, she wanted him.

Every inch of him.

And for the first time in a long, long time, she didn't feel like a woman just surviving.

She felt wanted. Desired. *Seen.*

And she wasn't going to pretend otherwise.

Not tonight.

Not with Theo.

CHAPTER 6

Theo couldn't believe this was happening. He was kissing Emma. *Emma.* His best friend from high school. The girl he'd crushed on for years. The one who starred in all his late-night fantasies, the one he never thought he'd ever truly touch.

But now?

Now she was in his arms, beneath him, kissing him back with hunger and heat and years of something left unsaid.

Her lips parted, and her sapphire eyes met his, stormy with desire. His heart hammered, but it was her voice, soft and breathless, that broke him.

"Theo..."

"Tell me you want this," he whispered against her mouth, needing the words more than he expected. "Tell me this isn't just a game."

A beat. Then her hand slid up his chest, her fingers curling around his neck.

"Yes, Theo," she breathed. "I want you. I've always wanted you... I just didn't know it until now."

The words crashed over him, and suddenly, nothing else mattered.

The world fell away, just the two of them, the dim light of the jet cabin, the hum of snowstorm winds swirling around them outside. Inside, something was catching fire.

He swept the cards off the table in one swift motion and lifted her onto the cool wood surface. She laughed, sharp, breathy, unguarded. He'd never heard anything sweeter.

Then he leaned in and kissed her again.

The moment their lips met, something shifted. All the years of quiet friendship, of stolen glances and unspoken thoughts, dissolved into heat and skin and urgency. They weren't just reconnecting. They were *reclaiming* something they didn't even know they'd lost.

He fumbled with her buttons, not caring as they popped and scattered. She arched beneath his hands, breath catching, eyes never leaving his. She was gorgeous, God, more than he remembered, and real. This wasn't a dream. This wasn't a fantasy. This was Emma. *His* Emma.

He kissed a trail down her throat, across her collarbone, and down to her bare skin. Her fingers tugged at his belt, sliding open his jeans, and when he stepped back and stripped down, her eyes widened, and she smiled, a slow, wicked smile that went straight to his gut.

Turning toward her, his cock was hard as she gazed at him.

"Wow," she said as her hand reached for him. Her fingers brushed the head and he knew he wouldn't last long. So he'd fulfill his first fantasy.

He caught her hand, his voice hoarse as he pulled her panties down. "Not yet."

She blinked. "Why not?"

"Because I've waited years for this," he said. "And I'm not going to rush a second of it."

When he finally touched her, really touched her, it wasn't

about control, it was about reverence. About memorizing her. About showing her, in every movement, what she meant to him.

The years fell away as he explored every inch of her with his hands, his mouth, his breath. Every sound she made became a kind of music. Every tremble of her body beneath him was a revelation. She'd always been brave, always been bright. But now she was wild and open and achingly vulnerable.

And she was his.

The moment built between them with an intensity that left him breathless. He kissed her like she was his salvation. Like he'd been waiting a lifetime for this night. And maybe he had.

He whispered her name against her skin, again and again, like a promise.

They were naked and her body was exactly what his fantasies had been filled with. Long silky legs, a narrow waist, and full breasts he couldn't wait to taste.

Nudging her legs, he gazed down at her sweet pussy and a moan escaped him. First things first. He had to taste her.

Gripping her knees, he spread them apart as his fingers delved into her and his face found her center. Taking a deep breath, he inhaled her scent and then his tongue flicked her little button as he began to lick her.

"Theo," she cried, her hands clenching. "Oh."

With his teeth, he nipped her clit, and she squirmed on the table as his tongue stroked her folds. She smelled sweet and tasted so good as his fingers plunged inside her and his lips continued to pummel her clit.

Her hands reached for his head and she pulled him in closer, gripping handfuls of his hair. She clung to him and he gave her all his attention. How many years had he dreamed of this moment? How long had he wanted her in his life? By his side?

To say he loved her would be an understatement. He adored her, worshipped her, and wanted to make her his wife.

Hopefully, tonight was just the beginning. Hopefully tonight, she would realize the emotions between them. Hopefully after tonight, she would never leave him again.

While his tongue worked its magic, his fingers twisted and turned inside her, making sure she felt the magic between them.

"Theo," she screamed and her body convulsed around him.

Raising his head, he glanced at her as she lay there, eyes closed, her breathing labored.

Crawling up her body, his mouth trailed kisses up her stomach and chest until he reached her nipples where his tongue laved the tight little kernels.

"Damn, Theo," she said with a gasp. Her hands reached for his penis and he grabbed them.

"Oh no, tonight is all about you," he said, wanting this time to be the best experience she'd ever had.

Right now, he didn't want her touching him because he feared he would explode in her hands and he had to be inside her. To feel her body wrapped around his cock.

His lips found her nipple and he sucked it into his mouth, nipping it with his teeth, but he had to taste her lips once again. Her full, luscious mouth he'd been staring at all night wondering how she would taste.

Coming up, his mouth found hers and he kissed her, raising her arms over her head as he held her hands with his.

Tonight he would claim her. Make her his. Tonight, he wanted to last a lifetime.

When their bodies finally came together, it wasn't just about need, it was about *knowing*. About years of watching her from across the school hallway. About feeling like he'd never be enough, and now finally realizing he was everything she wanted.

She gasped his name, and he held on. Held back. Tried to make it last.

It was too much and not enough. He was inside her, and yet he still couldn't get close enough. Couldn't get deep enough to touch the parts of her he'd been aching to reach for years.

Every sound she made shattered something inside him. Every whispered plea carved him open.

When they came undone, together, it felt less like surrender and more like coming home.

After, they didn't speak for a long moment. Just lay there on the table, tangled up in breath and skin and something brand new, something terrifyingly tender.

She looked up at him with wide, searching eyes. Her hair a mess, cheeks flushed, lips swollen from his kiss.

"That was…" she whispered.

He bent down and kissed her forehead. "More than I ever imagined."

Still wordless, he scooped her up, not bothering to dress, and carried her toward the bedroom.

"Where are we going?" she asked, drowsy but glowing.

"I'm not finished with you," he murmured into her hair. "We did the table. Now it's time for the bed."

She laughed, soft and sleepy, and it wrapped around his heart like silk.

In the hallway, he stopped and kissed the curve of her neck, slow and deliberate.

"I don't want this to be one night," he said, barely audible.

Her hand found his chest, resting over his heart.

"I don't either."

And in that moment, Theo knew, this wasn't just about sex. This was something bigger. Something that had waited long enough.

He just hoped she'd be brave enough to stay.

CHAPTER 7

The metallic patter of sleet against aluminum pulled her from sleep. For a moment, she lay still, disoriented by the unfamiliar weight of contentment in her chest. The sound was oddly rhythmic, like someone tossing handfuls of gravel against the fuselage, reminding her exactly where she was.

Stranded. On Theo's private plane. In the middle of a blizzard that showed no signs of mercy.

Then she remembered everything else.

Theo.

She turned her head on the pillow, her hair spilling across Egyptian cotton that probably cost more than her monthly rent. He lay sprawled on his stomach beside her, one arm flung across the space she'd occupied, as if even in sleep he'd been reaching for her. Dark hair fell across his forehead in a way that made him look younger, almost like the boy she'd known in high school. In sleep, his features held an unexpected vulnerability, the sharp jaw softened, the intensity that usually crackled around him dimmed to something gentler. Those emerald eyes that had burned into her last night were hidden beneath dark lashes that were frankly unfair on a man.

This was the man who'd kept her up until dawn. The man whose hands had mapped every inch of her body with a reverence that made her breath catch even now, hours later. The man who'd made her forget every rule she'd ever set for herself about casual encounters and protecting her heart.

The skinny boy from AP Chemistry, the one who'd helped her cram for the SATs and shared his lunch when she forgot hers, had become someone who knew exactly how to make her forget her own name.

And that terrified her more than any exam she'd ever faced.

Last night had started so innocently. Cards and champagne and the kind of laughter that made your stomach hurt. Then his hand had brushed hers reaching for cards, and something had shifted. The air had gotten thicker. His eyes had darkened. Playing rummy, she'd deliberately lost, so he would remove her jeans.

And before she knew it, they were tearing at each other's clothes, desperate and hungry, and she'd found herself laid out on the table, with him worshipping her body.

She'd never done anything like that. Never been that reckless, that consumed by want. But with Theo, everything felt different. Natural. Like they'd been building toward this moment for years without realizing it, all those study sessions and late-night conversations just foreplay for something inevitable.

Too perfect, that was the problem. This easy intimacy, the way their bodies fit together like complementary pieces, how he somehow knew what she needed before she asked, it was the kind of perfect that didn't last. The kind that existed in snow globes and airport novels. The kind that made you reckless enough to believe in fairy tales.

And she was too practical for fairy tales. She was a med student, for god's sake. She dealt in anatomy and pathology and the brutal reality of the human body. Not romance. Not this aching feeling in her chest that felt dangerously close to something she wasn't ready to name.

She slipped from the bed before she could do something stupid like wake him with kisses and confess feelings she didn't fully understand herself.

The floor was cold beneath her bare feet as she padded into his bathroom. It was twice the size of the one she'd showered in yesterday, all gleaming fixtures and heated floors and the kind of marble that belonged in Italian villas. She caught her reflection in the mirror, hair wild, lips still slightly swollen, a faint mark on her collarbone where his mouth had been particularly insistent, and barely recognized herself.

She looked like a woman who'd been thoroughly loved.

The thought made her stomach flip.

She turned the shower as hot as it would go and stepped under the spray, letting the water pound against her shoulders. Maybe it would wash away this dangerous feeling blooming in her chest. Maybe the steam would burn out the fantasy before it could take root.

The glass door opened with a soft click.

"Good morning." Theo's voice was rough with sleep, gravelly and intimate in a way that sent heat spiraling through her. His hair was adorably mussed, sticking up in directions that testified to what they'd done last night. Water immediately began sluicing down his chest, highlighting every ridge of muscle, every line of that body she now knew as well as her own. "Mind if I join you?"

Her mouth went dry. She absolutely minded, because this was too domestic, too couple-like, too much of everything she was trying not to want. But what came out was, "I think you already have."

He grinned, that slow smile that transformed his entire face, and reached for her. But she caught his wrist, some instinct for self-preservation making her take control. Two could play at this game. If this was just physical, just a snow-day fling between old friends, then she could keep it there. Keep it in her hands.

Literally.

She grabbed the bar of soap and began working it into a lather, her hands sliding deliberately slow across his shoulders. His skin was hot beneath her palms, slick with water. She traced the breadth of his shoulders, down his arms where she could feel the flex of muscle, over the plane of his chest where his heart beat steady and strong. His breath hitched when she traced the cut of his abs, following that trail of hair that arrowed downward, then moved lower still.

"You're trouble," he muttered, his voice strained.

"You have no idea." She let her nails graze his inner thigh, watching his pupils dilate until only a thin ring of green remained. The soap made her hands slick as she wrapped them around his length, feeling him twitch and harden further in her grip. His sharp intake of breath sent a thrill through her, this power, this ability to reduce him to gasps and groans.

But before she could establish any real rhythm, he spun her around with a growl. Her palms hit the tile wall, and she barely had time to gasp before he was pressed against her back, his mouth hot on her neck, teeth grazing that sensitive spot just below her ear.

"Theo—"

"I've got you, sweetheart." His voice was pure sin, low and promising. His hand slid between her legs, fingers finding exactly the right spot with the kind of precision that suggested he'd memorized her body in a single night. "Is this what you want?"

She could only moan as he pushed inside her, filling her completely, stretching her in a way that was just the right side of too much. His other hand splayed across her stomach, holding her steady against him as he moved, slow at first, then building. The combination of sensations, his fingers working her clit in tight circles, the stretch and slide of him inside her, the hot water cascading over them both, the steam making everything hazy and dreamlike, built into something overwhelming.

"Please," she gasped, not even sure what she was asking for. More? Less? Never stop?

"I know, sweetheart. I've got you." His rhythm intensified, and she felt herself spiraling toward the edge of something vast. "Let go. I've got you."

The permission was all she needed. When the orgasm hit, it shattered through her with such force that her legs nearly gave out, waves of pleasure radiating from her core to her fingertips. She heard herself cry out his name, heard it echo off the tile, and distantly registered that the crew probably heard it too. She couldn't bring herself to care.

Theo caught her, one arm banding across her chest, holding her against him as he found his own release with a groan that reverberated through his chest and into her back.

They stood there for a long moment, breathing hard, steam swirling around them like clouds. Her forehead pressed against the cool tile, his forehead pressed against her shoulder blade. She could feel his heart hammering against her spine, as frantic as her own.

He turned her in his arms, gentle now, and tucked a wet strand of hair behind her ear. His expression was softer than she'd ever seen it, open in a way that made her chest tighten. "I woke up and you were gone."

There was something in his voice, not quite hurt, but close. A vulnerability that matched her own.

"I needed a shower." It came out more defensive than she'd intended, walls slamming back into place.

He studied her face, his thumb tracing her cheekbone with a tenderness that felt more dangerous than the passion had. She had the uncomfortable feeling he could read every thought she was trying to hide, could see right through her deflections to the terrified woman underneath.

Instead of calling her on it, he reached for the soap. "Let me."

What followed was somehow more intimate than what came before. His hands were gentle as he washed her, taking care with every inch of skin. He traced the curve of her shoulders, the dip of her waist, the length of her legs. No man had ever done this. They usually rolled over and fell asleep, or made excuses to leave, or checked their phones while she gathered her clothes. But Theo cleaned her like it mattered, like she mattered, and something in her chest cracked open despite her best efforts to keep it sealed.

"Better?" he asked softly, rinsing soap from her skin.

"Yeah." Her voice came out small, young, nothing like the confident woman she tried to project.

"Good. Now I'm starving, and if Jenny hasn't made coffee yet, I'm filing a formal complaint with the aviation board." He kissed her forehead, just a soft press of lips that shouldn't have meant anything but somehow meant everything, and stepped out of the shower, grabbing towels for them both. "Your suitcase is still in the living room. Want me to grab it?"

"That would be great, thanks."

He paused at the door, a wicked gleam sparking in those emerald eyes. "You know, if I had my way, you wouldn't need clothes at all today. I'd keep you naked and in bed until this storm passed."

Heat flooded her cheeks even as her body responded to the suggestion with embarrassing enthusiasm. "We have a crew on this plane, Theo. And it's freezing outside. And I have studying to do."

"A man can dream." He winked. "Be right back."

Alone, she pressed her palms to the cool marble counter and met her own eyes in the mirror. Her pupils were dilated, her skin flushed pink from the heat and the exertion, and something else entirely. She looked like a woman on the edge of falling.

No. She looked like a woman already halfway down.

When he brought her suitcase, she caught his wrist before he could leave. The question tumbled out before she could stop it, vulnerable and afraid. "Theo. Is this for real?"

He set the suitcase down and cupped her face, his thumb stroking her cheekbone, his eyes searching hers. "Only time will tell."

It wasn't the answer she wanted. She wanted declarations and promises and certainty. But maybe it was the honest one. Maybe it was all either of them could offer when they'd known each other for half their lives but only really seen each other for a single day.

An hour later, she sat curled in one of the leather armchairs, her anatomy textbook propped on her knees. She'd read the same paragraph about the brachial plexus three times without retaining a single word. Across the cabin, Theo typed rapidly on his laptop, his brow furrowed in concentration, completely absorbed in whatever business deal or market analysis demanded his attention.

This, too, felt familiar, the companionable silence, each of them focused on their own work. They'd studied like this in high school, sprawled across his bedroom floor or tucked into corner booths at the diner, testing each other on vocab words and formulas. She'd quiz him on historical dates; he'd drill her on physics equations.

When had comfortable become intoxicating?

She glanced out the window. Snow fell in thick, relentless sheets, already piled three feet high on the tarmac, transforming the airport into something from a snow globe. The planes on either side of them were barely visible through the white curtain. They weren't going anywhere soon, not today, maybe not tomorrow. The thought should have frustrated her.

But instead, she felt a guilty flutter of relief.

More time. More of this. More of him.

She watched Theo work, cataloging the little things she'd never noticed before. The way he absently ran his hand through his hair when he was thinking, making it stick up even more. The sharp focus in his eyes when he was concentrating. The slight smile when he typed something he was particularly pleased with.

Twenty-four hours ago, he'd been her oldest friend. Someone safe and familiar and comfortable, like a well-worn sweater.

Now he was the man who'd made her scream his name against a shower wall. The man whose touch left her aching for more, even when she was still sore from the last time. The man who was starting to feel dangerously necessary, like oxygen or caffeine or all the other things she couldn't function without.

She'd gone from friends to lovers in one snow-stranded night, and she had no idea how to go back. Wasn't sure she wanted to. Wasn't sure what would happen when they finally left this plane and returned to reality.

Outside, the storm showed no signs of stopping. Inside, something equally powerful had already begun. And just like the blizzard, she suspected there was no stopping it now.

CHAPTER 8

Theo's fingers stilled on the keyboard.

Across the cabin, Emma had fallen asleep on the couch, her anatomy textbook sliding off her lap onto the floor. She lay curled on her side, one hand tucked beneath her cheek like a child, auburn hair spilling across the leather cushion. Even in sleep, she was beautiful, those dark lashes fanned against porcelain skin, her lips slightly parted, the gentle rise and fall of her breath creating a rhythm he found himself matching.

He should keep working. He had three contracts to review before the holiday break, a merger proposal that required his signature, and a conference call scheduled for tomorrow morning that he'd probably have to reschedule due to the weather. His inbox was a disaster, his assistant had sent four increasingly frantic messages, and the Tokyo office was waiting on his decision about the new facility.

But he couldn't tear his eyes away from her.

God, she looked cold.

He rose from his chair, muscles protesting after two hours hunched over his laptop, and retrieved a cashmere throw from the storage compartment. As he draped it over her, tucking it gently around her shoulders, she made a small sound of contentment and burrowed deeper into the couch. Something in his chest expanded painfully.

This woman. This infuriating, brilliant, beautiful woman who'd walked back into his life less than twenty-four hours ago and turned his entire world sideways.

He'd tried to forget her. God knows he'd tried. In college, he'd dated other girls, smart girls, pretty girls, girls who should have been perfect for him. But none of them had been Emma. None of them had challenged him the way she did, made him laugh until his stomach hurt, or looked at him like he was just Theo, not the nerd that everyone made fun of, but a real human being..

When he'd built his company from the ground up, determined to make something of himself, she'd been there in the back of his mind. A ghost of what-ifs and might-have-beens.

And now she was here. On his plane. In his bed.

In his heart, if he was being honest with himself.

Seeing her at that rental car counter last night had felt like divine intervention. Like the universe had decided to give him a second chance and wrapped it in a blizzard with a bow on top. And then the plane, the storm, the cards, it had all led to the best night of his life.

Better than any business deal he'd ever closed. Better than the day he'd made his first million. Better than anything.

Because with Emma, he didn't have to pretend. He didn't have to be charming, Theodore Whitmore, the boy wonder who'd turned his game into an empire before thirty. He could just be Theo, the kid who'd helped her study for the SATs.

He returned to his chair, but instead of opening his laptop, he just watched her sleep. Her nose wrinkled slightly, and she shifted, the blanket slipping down to reveal the curve of her shoulder. He knew that shoulder now. Knew the taste of it, the softness of it, the way she shivered when he kissed the sensitive hollow above her collarbone.

Last night had been explosive. This morning in the shower, Christ, he was getting hard just thinking about it. The way she'd taken control at first, her soapy hands driving him out of his mind. The way she'd gasped his name when he'd made her come. The way she'd looked at him afterward, vulnerable and scared and hopeful all at once.

She felt it too. This thing between them. He knew she did.

But she was also terrified. He'd seen it in her eyes this morning when she'd asked if this was real. She was protecting herself, waiting for him to disappoint her, to reveal that this was just a fling or a game or something that would evaporate when they returned to reality.

If only she knew.

He wanted everything with her. Marriage. Kids. A house with a yard and a dog and family dinners and all the mundane, beautiful moments that made up a life. He wanted to wake up next to her every morning for the next sixty years. He wanted to take her to Italy and watch her eyes light up at the art. He wanted to sit across from her at breakfast and steal bites of her toast. He wanted to fight with her about what to watch on TV and make up in increasingly creative ways.

He wanted it all.

The realization should have terrified him. He was thirty years old, for Christ's sake. He'd built a company, managed hundreds of employees, and negotiated deals worth millions. He was supposed to be rational, logical, strategic.

But there was nothing rational about what he felt for Emma.

And he didn't care.

His laptop screen had gone dark. He tapped the trackpad and pulled up a new browser window, then paused, fingers hovering over the keys. This was insane. He'd known, really known, she was back in his life for less than a day.

But when you know, you know. His father had proposed to his mother after two weeks. His grandfather had eloped with his grandmother after a month. The Whitmore men didn't do anything halfway, especially when it came to love.

He typed "engagement rings" into the search bar.

For the next hour, he scrolled through hundreds of options, dismissing most immediately. Too gaudy. Too plain. Too trendy. Too traditional. Nothing felt right, nothing felt like Emma, until he found it.

The ring materialized on his screen and his breath caught.

It was perfect. A stunning oval diamond, at least three carats, surrounded by a halo of smaller stones that made it sparkle like captured starlight. The platinum band was elegant and simple, with tiny diamonds set into the sides. Classic but not boring. Timeless but not stuffy. Sophisticated but not pretentious.

Emma.

It was Emma in ring form.

His hand shook slightly as he clicked through to the jeweler's website. Exclusive. By appointment only. Custom designs. The kind of place that didn't list prices because if you had to ask, you couldn't afford it.

Good thing money wasn't an issue.

He glanced at Emma, still sleeping peacefully, then back at the ring. Was he really doing this? Was he really about to spend five figures on an engagement ring for a woman he hadn't even dated yet?

Yes. Yes, he absolutely was.

Because this wasn't just any woman. This was Emma. His Emma. The girl who'd shared her lunch with him when he forgot his. The girl who'd stayed up all night helping him study for chemistry even though she had her own exam the next day. The girl who'd believed in him before he'd believed in himself.

The woman who'd looked at him last night like he hung the moon.

The woman he was going to marry.

He pulled out his phone and dialed the number listed on the

website. It rang four times before a cultured voice answered. "Rothschild & Sons, how may I assist you?"

"I need an engagement ring," Theo said, keeping his voice low so he wouldn't wake Emma. "The oval solitaire with the halo setting. Platinum band. I'm looking at it on your website right now."

"Ah, yes. Excellent choice, sir. That particular piece is quite extraordinary. When would you like to schedule an appointment to view it?"

"I don't. I want to buy it. Now. Tonight."

A pause. "Sir, that ring is $90,000. Perhaps you'd like to—"

"I'm aware of the price. I'll wire the money tonight. I need it shipped overnight to Whitefish, Montana." He rattled off the address of his family's ranch.

Another pause, longer this time. "Sir, I'm afraid overnight shipping during the holidays, particularly given the current weather conditions—"

"I'll pay whatever it costs. Twenty thousand for expedited shipping. Thirty. Name your price."

"I... I'll need to speak with my manager."

"You do that. I'll hold."

The line went silent except for tinny classical music. Theo waited, his heart hammering in his chest like he was closing a billion-dollar deal instead of buying jewelry. This was different, though. More important. The stakes were higher than any business transaction.

This was his future.

The voice returned. "Sir? We can have it delivered to Whitefish by the end of the day on December 26th, weather permitting. The total, including expedited shipping and insurance, will be $115,000."

"Done. I'll have my bank wire the funds within the hour. Email me the confirmation."

He provided his information, hung up, and immediately

called his banker. By the time he'd finished arranging the transfer, his hands were sweating and his heart was racing like he'd run a marathon.

Holy shit. He'd just bought an engagement ring.

For Emma.

Who might say no.

The thought sent ice through his veins. What if she wasn't ready? What if this was too much, too soon? What if she thought he was crazy or impulsive or—

No. No, he couldn't think like that. This was right. He knew it in his bones.

But the ring wouldn't arrive for days, and suddenly he couldn't bear the thought of waiting that long to ask her. The question was burning in his throat, demanding to be spoken.

He needed a placeholder, something to give her now, today, this moment before he lost his nerve.

Theo opened a new document and pulled up the photo of the ring from the jeweler's website. He saved it, opened his photo editing software, and spent the next twenty minutes carefully cropping and adjusting until he had a clean image of just the ring. He printed it on the cabin's color printer—thank God for first-world amenities, and stared at the result.

A picture of a ring. On printer paper.

It was ridiculous. It was probably the least romantic proposal prop in the history of proposals. But it would have to do.

He found Jenny in the galley, pulling a tray of something that smelled incredible from the oven. "Can you help me with something?"

She looked up, her eyes twinkling with amusement. "Of course, Mr. Whitmore."

"Call me Theo. Please. And I need..." He held up the printed ring photo, feeling his cheeks heat. "I need to make this look like an actual ring."

Jenny's eyes widened, then her face split into a huge grin. "Oh my God. Are you—"

"Yes. But the real ring won't arrive for days, and I can't wait, so I need..." He gestured helplessly at the paper.

"Say no more." Jenny dried her hands and pulled open a drawer, producing scissors, tape, and a small jewelry box she apparently kept stashed for emergencies. "I've got you."

Together, they carefully cut out the ring image and fashioned it into something that could almost pass for a real ring if you squinted and didn't look too closely. Jenny found a twist-tie and used it to create a makeshift band, then nestled the whole thing into the jewelry box.

"It's terrible," Theo said, staring at their creation.

"It's perfect," Jenny corrected. "Trust me. She won't care about the ring. She'll care about what it means."

He hoped she was right.

Captain Reynolds appeared in the galley doorway, charts in hand and a grim expression on his weathered face. "Sir, we need to discuss the weather."

Theo's stomach sank. "Don't tell me it's getting worse."

"Not worse. Just not better. This system is stalled over Montana. We're looking at another thirty-six to forty-eight hours minimum before we can safely take off. Maybe longer."

Two days ago, that news would have destroyed him. He'd had plans, Christmas Eve with his family, skiing in Whitefish, the annual Whitmore holiday party that his mother spent months planning. Being stuck in an airport, even a private one, even in his own plane, would have been a nightmare.

But that was before Emma.

Now? Now he wanted to thank the storm gods personally.

"That's fine," he said, and meant it. "We're comfortable here. We have supplies?"

"A week's worth, easy," Jenny confirmed. "More if we're careful."

"Then we wait it out." He turned to Reynolds and Jenny, who were both trying not to smirk at him. "I know you both have families. Once we get to Whitefish, take the plane. Spend Christmas with your people. That's an order."

Jenny's eyes shimmered. "Thank you, sir."

"Theo," he corrected automatically. "And thank you both for taking care of us. I know this isn't how you wanted to spend your holiday either."

Reynolds clapped him on the shoulder. "If I may speak freely, sir, Theo, we're happy for you. Emma seems like a wonderful woman."

"She is." Theo's chest tightened with emotion. "She really is."

After they left, he stood in the galley for a moment, the makeshift ring box in his hand, and let himself imagine it. Emma saying yes. Emma wearing his ring, the real one, not this ridiculous paper substitute. Emma becoming Emma Whitmore.

Emma as his wife.

The thought filled him with a joy so intense it was almost painful.

He returned to the main cabin. Emma was still sleeping, the blanket wrapped around her like a cocoon. The late afternoon light filtered through the windows, painting her in shades of gold. She'd be awake soon, probably hungry. Jenny was making dinner, something special, she'd said with a knowing wink.

He could ask her tonight. Over dinner. Or maybe after, during a movie. They could curl up on the couch with hot chocolate and watch something sappy and Christmas-themed, and when the moment was right, he'd pull out the box and—

And what? Give her a paper ring and hope she didn't laugh in his face?

God, he was an idiot. A besotted, impulsive, reckless idiot.

But he was an idiot in love.

He tucked the ring box into his pocket and returned to his laptop. There were emails to answer, decisions to make, a business empire that wouldn't run itself. But his mind was elsewhere, spinning fantasies of a future that suddenly seemed within reach.

Emma stirred, her eyes fluttering open. She blinked in confusion for a moment before her gaze found his. A slow smile spread across her face, sleepy and warm and so beautiful it hurt.

"Hey," she murmured, her voice husky from sleep. "How long was I out?"

"Couple hours. You were exhausted."

She sat up, pushing her hair out of her face, and the blanket slipped down. "You covered me?"

"You looked cold."

Something soft crossed her expression. "Thank you."

"Always," he said, and meant it in ways she didn't yet understand. Always. Forever. For the rest of his life, if she'd let him.

The ring box burned in his pocket like a secret, like a promise, like the future he was about to reach for with both hands.

Soon, he told himself. Soon he'd ask her.

And God willing, she'd say yes.

CHAPTER 9

"Mom, I'm safe," Emma said for the third time, pressing the phone closer to her ear as she moved toward the plane's small window. Outside, snow continued its relentless assault on the tarmac. "I'm staying with Theo. You remember him from high school."

Silence stretched across the line, so long Emma wondered if they'd lost connection.

"Yes," her mother finally said, her voice carrying that particular tone that meant she knew something Emma didn't. "I remember Theo. He had a terrible crush on you, sweetheart. I don't think you ever realized that boy was absolutely crazy about you."

Emma's stomach dropped. She stared at her phone like it had betrayed her. "What?"

"Theo. He was in love with you. We all saw it."

"No." Emma shook her head even though her mother couldn't see. "We were just friends. That's all we ever were."

But even as she said it, memories flickered through her mind like an old film reel. Theo always offering to carry her books. Theo bringing her favorite candy bar when she was stressed about exams. Theo looking away quickly whenever she caught him staring. Theo's jaw tightening when she talked about other boys.

Oh God.

"You thought you were just friends," her mother said gently. "But I knew differently. We all did. He was a sweet boy. I always liked him."

Emma's mind reeled. All those conversations they'd had rating boys at school—assigning them numbers based on whether they'd ever ask her out. Nine meant good chance, one meant no way in hell. She'd dissected every interaction with every guy in their class while Theo sat there, nodding and agreeing and never once suggesting she look at the boy sitting right in front of her.

Why hadn't he said something? Why hadn't he stopped her?

Because you would have panicked and pulled away, a voice whispered in her head. Because you weren't ready to see him that way.

"Emma? You still there?"

"Yeah, I'm here." She pressed her forehead against the cold window. "I just... I had no idea."

In high school, she'd been the nerdy twin. Amelia got the dates and the attention while Emma got good grades and a reputation for being intimidatingly smart. She'd found frog dissection fascinating when other girls were squeamish. She'd corrected teachers who made mistakes. She'd punched Tommy Morrison in the face for picking on a freshman and hadn't regretted it even when she got suspended.

Not exactly prom queen material.

But Theo had never seemed to mind. He'd studied with her, laughed with her, sat with her at lunch when no one else would. She'd thought he was just being nice.

Apparently, she'd been blind.

"When did this attraction between us actually begin?" she murmured, more to herself than her mother.

"Sweetheart, I can't answer that for you. But be careful, okay? I always thought you two went well together, but you're in a vulnerable position right now."

If only her mother knew just how vulnerable.

Emma glanced back toward the living area where Theo sat working, his dark hair falling forward over his face as he focused on his laptop. Her chest tightened with an emotion she wasn't ready to name.

This morning had been perfect. They'd argued good-naturedly about politics over coffee, debating education policy and healthcare reform with the kind of intellectual sparring she'd missed since leaving school. He'd challenged her assumptions about homeschooling. She'd opened his eyes to why so many doctors now came from abroad—American kids drowning in debt they couldn't afford to accumulate.

The conversation had been stimulating. Engaging.

Sexy, in a way she'd never experienced with anyone else.

And then they'd ended up in the shower again, steam and soap and hands that knew exactly where to touch. It was becoming a pattern. Talk, laugh, touch, explode. Like they were making up for fifteen years of lost time in a matter of days.

"I'll be home just as soon as planes start flying," Emma said, pulling herself back to the conversation. "How about Amelia? Have you heard from her?"

"Yes." Her mother's voice brightened. "She and Olivia are both stranded too. Olivia says she's safe but won't tell me where. Amelia's with a paramedic, apparently. Don't ask me why because I have no idea."

"So I'm not the last one home?"

"No, it's just me and your father so far. Everyone else is trying to get here but stuck in this awful weather."

Something in her mother's tone made Emma pause. There

was an undercurrent there, something weighted and unspoken. "Mom, are you all right? Is Dad okay?"

"We're both fine, dear." But her voice had that careful quality it took on when she was hiding something. "I just want my children home for Christmas. I have something I need to tell you all, but that can wait until everyone's together."

Dread pooled in Emma's stomach. "Mom—"

"It's nothing bad, sweetheart. Just something that needs to be said in person. With everyone there."

Emma knew that tone. Her mother wouldn't budge until she was ready. Pushing would only make her dig in harder. "Okay. I'll call you as soon as the airport reopens."

"Be careful," her mother said again, softer this time. "I still say Theo had a crush on you. But he's a good man. I think you're safe with him."

"Love you, Mom."

"Love you too, baby."

The line went dead.

Emma stood there for a long moment, phone pressed to her chest, staring out at the blizzard. Three days. Most storms blew through in twenty-four hours, but this monster had parked itself over Montana and refused to leave. The snow fell in thick sheets, already piled so high she couldn't see the ground anymore.

When would it end?

And more importantly, was she ready for it to end?

The thought sent a flutter through her stomach. Once the planes started flying, this bubble would burst. They'd return to the real world, where Theo was a gaming mogul with a company to run and she was a PA student with rotations and exams. Where they lived in different cities and had different lives, and couldn't spend entire days in bed talking about everything and nothing.

The idea of losing this made her chest ache.

She turned from the window and found Theo exactly where

she'd left him—hunched over his laptop, fingers flying across the keyboard, completely absorbed in whatever he was working on. Code, probably. Some intricate string of programming language that made sense only to him.

He'd always been like this. Even in freshman science class, he'd been the one solving problems while everyone else was still reading the instructions. Biology had been her strongest subject, but even there she'd had to work twice as hard to keep up with him.

The man was brilliant. Legitimately, frustratingly brilliant.

And apparently, he'd been in love with her.

The knowledge sat strange and warm in her chest. How had she missed it? How had she been so blind?

She studied him now, really studied him. The way his hair fell forward when he concentrated. The strong line of his jaw. The broad shoulders that filled out his shirt in ways they definitely hadn't in high school. The elegant movements of his hands across the keyboard.

God, she wanted him.

Not just physically, though that was certainly there. She wanted to know what he was working on. Wanted to understand the games he created, the empire he'd built. She'd never been much for video games, they'd always seemed like a waste of time when she could be studying, but suddenly she wanted to know everything about his world.

She'd never considered him for a boyfriend in high school. But now, watching him work with that intense focus she remembered so well, all she could think about was distracting him.

Her feet carried her across the cabin before she made a conscious decision to move.

He looked up as she approached, his expression softening immediately. Those emerald eyes warmed in a way that made her pulse quicken. "Emma?"

She didn't answer. Instead, she reached out and caught his

chin, tilting his face up toward hers. Maybe he'd had a crush on her years ago, but now she was the one consumed with need. Now she was the one who couldn't think straight when he was in the room.

Her lips found his, and she poured everything into the kiss, all the confusion and desire and terrifying hope that had been building since the moment she saw him at that rental counter. She kissed him like she was claiming him, like she was answering a question he'd been too afraid to ask.

His response was immediate. He stood, pulling her flush against him, one hand tangling in her hair while the other splayed across the small of her back. The laptop clattered forgotten onto the chair cushion.

"Bedroom," she breathed against his mouth. "Now."

He didn't need to be told twice.

They stumbled toward the back of the plane, hands already working at buttons and zippers, leaving a trail of discarded clothing in their wake. She kicked off her shoes somewhere near the galley. His shirt landed on the floor outside the bathroom. By the time they reached the bedroom, they were mostly naked and laughing breathlessly at their own urgency.

Theo backed her toward the bed, his hands everywhere, his mouth trailing fire down her neck. "What brought this on?" he murmured against her collarbone. "Not that I'm complaining."

"I just..." She gasped as his teeth grazed her shoulder. "I wanted you."

"Good." He lifted his head, his eyes dark with desire. "Because I always want you."

He pulled her down onto the bed, and then he was settling between her thighs, and she was wrapping her legs around his waist, and they were moving together like they'd been doing this for years instead of days.

No condom again.

The rational part of her brain, the med student part, the

responsible part, screamed a warning. But she pushed it away. This was Theo. Her Theo. The boy who'd loved her when she didn't know how to love herself. The man who was teaching her that maybe, just maybe, she was worth loving.

Later, she'd worry about consequences. Later, she'd be sensible.

Right now, she just wanted to feel.

He moved inside her with a rhythm that was becoming familiar, each thrust deliberate and deep. His eyes never left hers, and there was something in his gaze that made her heart stutter, something raw and vulnerable and absolutely terrifying.

"Emma," he breathed, and her name had never sounded like that before. Like a prayer. Like a promise.

"I'm here," she whispered back, her hands framing his face. "I'm right here."

The orgasm built slowly this time, a steady crescendo rather than an explosion. When it finally crashed over her, it felt different—less frantic, more profound. Like something was shifting between them, clicking into place.

Theo followed moments later with a groan, his forehead pressed to hers, his breath hot against her lips.

They lay tangled together afterward, hearts racing, skin damp with sweat. Outside, the storm continued its assault. Inside, Emma felt like she was in the eye of a different kind of storm entirely.

"Your mom called?" Theo asked eventually, his fingers tracing lazy patterns on her shoulder.

"Yeah. She wanted to make sure I was safe."

"What did you tell her?"

Emma hesitated. "That I was with you."

"And?"

"And she said she remembered you." Emma turned her head to look at him. "She said you had a crush on me in high school."

Theo went very still. "Did she now."

"Did you?"

For a long moment, he didn't answer. His fingers stilled on her shoulder. Then, quietly: "Yes."

Emma's breath caught. "Why didn't you tell me?"

"Because you weren't ready to hear it." He rolled onto his side to face her, his expression serious. "You were so busy trying to prove yourself, Emma. So focused on grades and college and becoming a doctor. You had this wall up, and I didn't want to be another thing putting pressure on you."

"So you just... waited?"

"I moved on," he corrected gently. "Or tried to. Dated other people. Built a life. But you were always there, in the back of my mind. And when I saw you at that rental counter..." He cupped her face, his thumb stroking her cheekbone. "It was like no time had passed at all."

Tears pricked Emma's eyes. "I was so blind."

"You were focused. There's a difference." He kissed her forehead. "And maybe we both needed to grow up before we were ready for this."

This. Whatever this was. This terrifying, exhilarating thing that felt like free-falling and coming home all at once.

Emma pressed her face into his chest, breathing him in. Outside, the blizzard raged on. Inside, wrapped in Theo's arms, she felt safer than she had in years.

And that scared her most of all.

CHAPTER 10

*L*ying in bed, Theo watched the snow fall past the window, fat, lazy flakes that seemed in no hurry to reach the ground. The kind of snow that made the world feel smaller, safer. Like nothing existed beyond this plane, this bed, this woman in his arms.

"How long is this storm going to last?" Emma asked.

Every muscle in his body tensed with the effort not to burst into song. *Let it snow, let it snow, let it snow.* God, he was turning into a sap. A rich, successful tech mogul reduced to humming Christmas carols because he didn't want reality to intrude.

"Frankly, it could go on forever as far as I'm concerned." The words came out rougher than he intended, weighted with a truth that scared him. He tightened his arms around her, feeling the warmth of her back against his chest, the silk of her hair under his chin.

These three days, stranded, snowbound, cut off from the world, had been the best of his life. And tomorrow it would end. Tomorrow, the weather forecast promised clear skies. The little airport would scramble to clear runways, and the rest of the world would come rushing back in.

Unless he could convince her not to let it end.

"You could fly with me to Whitefish," he said, keeping his voice casual even as his heart hammered against his ribs.

She licked her lips, that nervous tell he'd already memorized. "What are we doing, Theo?"

Such an easy question. Such a terrifying answer.

"We're falling in love." The words hung in the air between them, naked and honest. His pulse thundered in his ears. He wanted her to know everything, his feelings, his plans, the ring waiting in Whitefish, but he forced himself to wait. Just a little longer. Do this right. The way she deserved.

A smile bloomed across her face, and something in his chest cracked open.

"We've known each other for years and yet it's been quite a while since we've seen each other." She gazed up at him, those sapphire eyes, God, those eyes, sparkling with something that made his breath catch. "How do I know you're the same man?"

The same man. The skinny kid who'd been shoved into lockers. The nerd who'd coded his first game in the school library while Billy Raye and his crew made his life hell. That frightened boy who'd loved Emma from afar, too terrified to even dream she might look at him twice.

"I'm a better man," Theo said, and he'd never meant anything more. "I'm not the frightened, skinny kid the bullies loved to abuse. I'm a strong, smart man who knows what he wants in life." He paused, his throat tight. "I'm more than capable of defending myself, my wife, and most especially, my children."

My wife. My children. The words tasted like a promise on his tongue. Like a future he could almost touch.

Emma. He wanted Emma.

"What do you want in life?" she asked softly.

Theo's mind raced. Did he tell her everything? Confess that he'd bought a ring less than twenty-four hours ago?

This wasn't how he'd imagined proposing. Not in a plane bed

with rumpled sheets, snow falling outside, no grand gesture or perfect moment. But maybe that was exactly what made it right.

Not yet. Hold on just a little longer.

"It's simple what I want and yet, it's the best." His voice dropped, rough with emotion. "I want a wife and kids. I want to wake up on Christmas morning and hear my kids running down the stairs to see what Santa brought them."

The image was so vivid it hurt, a house filled with noise and laughter and love. Everything he'd never had growing up. Everything he'd built his empire to create.

"I want to buy my wife the biggest damn diamonds she'll let me. I want to take my family on trips. Watch my son play sports, if he wants to. Or maybe he's a nerd like me and we build video games together."

He could see it. A little boy with Emma's eyes, hunched over a keyboard beside him. Or maybe a daughter. Maybe both. A whole tribe of them.

"I want a family of my own, and I want to give them the best possible life."

When he glanced down, tears glistened on Emma's lashes like diamonds. His heart stopped.

"What do you want, Emma?"

Please. Please want the same thing.

"I want the same," she whispered. "But I want at least three kids, maybe four."

Relief crashed through him so hard he laughed, a sound that came from somewhere deep in his chest, somewhere that had been locked tight for years. He pulled her closer, inhaling the scent of her shampoo, feeling the steady beat of her heart.

"I was thinking five."

She grinned up at him, her nose crinkling in that way that made him want to kiss every inch of her face. "Five? Do you think I'm a broodmare?"

He leaned down and kissed her, tasting her laughter. "I want this, right here. Time with you. Time to spend cuddling and laughing and just having fun."

"I want a career," Emma said, and he heard the careful balance in her voice, the woman who'd fought for her education, her independence. "But not one that takes me away from my family all the time. Just when they're in school, and even then, only three days a week. More than anything I want to be a good mom and give my children the best life possible."

Theo's throat tightened. The image of Emma, belly rounded with his child, filled his mind with such intense longing it stole his breath. This felt so right. So perfectly, terrifyingly right.

"I want to live in a small town." Her voice grew stronger, more certain. "Raise my children away from the noise, the pollution, and all the danger I see everywhere. I want to be an overprotective momma bear."

A chuckle rumbled through his chest. Emma, fierce, loyal Emma, would be a force of nature as a mother. He pitied any bully who thought they'd get away with harming their kids. She'd protected him once, back when she hadn't owed him a damn thing. What would she do for children she'd carried and birthed and loved?

"Yes, a small town." He scooted down in the bed and rolled toward her, pulling her against him. Their faces were inches apart now, and he could count each freckle on her nose, see the gold flecks in her blue eyes. "I don't want this to end."

Emma bit her lip, and his stomach dropped at the worry creasing her forehead. "But I'm going to school in Denver. You work in New York City." Her voice wavered. "I'm just afraid this is a quick fling and then we'll go our separate ways."

No. The word screamed through his mind. *Not this time. Not you. Never you.*

"Do you want this to continue?"

"Yes," she breathed.

Thank God. Theo pulled the covers up to their necks as the temperature dropped with nightfall. Outside, the snow fell harder, coating the window in white.

"You won't be going to school forever," he told her, already calculating. He could work from anywhere. Could buy a house in Denver, split his time, and make it work. Whatever it took.

"No, but I haven't had much luck with long-distance relationships." Her voice went small, vulnerable in a way that made his chest ache. "In fact, I haven't had much luck at all with men."

A smile tugged at his lips despite the seriousness of the moment. "I've only had one serious relationship. Maybe we've been waiting for each other."

The truth of it settled over him like the snow outside, soft and inevitable. Every failed relationship, every lonely night, every time he'd wondered if he was broken somehow for not being able to feel what everyone else seemed to feel so easily. It had all been leading here. To her. To this.

"Maybe the universe put us here at this airport in Missoula because it's time for us to come together. Maybe we're meant for one another."

Emma reached up and ran her hand down his cheek, and Theo leaned into her touch like a man starved.

"You're a rich man." Her eyes searched his face. "How do you know I'm not after your money?"

His ex-girlfriend's face flashed through his mind, the way she'd lit up when he'd mentioned his portfolio, the designer bags that had multiplied in his closet, the subtle pressure to upgrade to a bigger penthouse, a flashier car. All the signs he'd ignored because he'd wanted so badly to believe someone could love him.

But Emma wasn't her. Emma was the girl who'd stood between him and a bully twice her size. Who'd risked her own reputation to save him. Who'd been his friend when being his friend earned her nothing but social exile.

"Are you?" he asked quietly.

"No," she said. "But how do you know?"

"You know when someone cares about you. You know when they jump on something you say. I don't know, but I've come to recognize the signs and I quickly distance myself from those types of people."

He traced the curve of her cheekbone with his thumb, memorizing the feel of her skin. "It's the ones that care about you that you want to cozy up to. I think you care about me."

Her smile was soft, almost shy. Her lashes swept down over those incredible eyes, and she sighed, a sound that went straight through him.

"That's what frightens me. I've not felt this way before. What if you decide tomorrow this was all a big mistake?"

Never. Theo moved his thumb over her bottom lip, felt it tremble beneath his touch. The vulnerability in her voice nearly undid him.

"I won't. Like I said earlier, I'm falling in love with you, Emma."

Am in love with you, he wanted to say. *Have been since high school. Will be until I die.*

"Given time, I think we could be right for one another."

Understatement of the century. She was perfect for him, had always been perfect for him. He just hadn't been ready for her until now. Hadn't been the man she deserved.

He thought of the ring hopefully waiting for him in Whitefish. Thought of asking her father for permission, old-fashioned, maybe, but Emma was old-fashioned in the ways that mattered. Thought of getting down on one knee and offering her everything he had, everything he was, everything he'd ever be.

Just as soon as they could get to Whitefish.

Emma reached up and pulled his head down to her, covering his lips with her own. The kiss was soft and sweet and tasted like promises. When she released him, her smile stole what was left of his breath.

"Thank you for letting me stay on your plane. Thank you for the best three days of my life."

Warmth flooded through him, the kind that started in his chest and radiated outward until his fingertips tingled with it. He rolled over on top of her, bracing his weight on his forearms, looking down at the woman who'd somehow become his entire world in seventy-two hours.

"You know we haven't been using a condom the last couple of days." His heart pounded as he said it. "What if you're pregnant? How would you feel?"

This was crazy. Reckless. Everything he'd never been in his careful, calculated life. But with Emma, he wanted to throw caution to the wind. Wanted to dive in headfirst and deal with the consequences later.

"Scared. Frightened. Excited," Emma said, her eyes wide and honest. "I'd like to finish my schooling, but I would be thrilled if I was expecting a child with you."

Yes. Theo grinned, unable to contain the joy that surged through him. That was exactly what he needed to hear. Exactly what his heart had been hoping for.

"Me too. In fact, I think we should practice a little more."

Her giggle made him feel like the luckiest man alive. She wrapped her arms around his neck, and he thought he could live forever in this moment, Emma beneath him, laughing and warm and his.

"How did I not know that you had a crush on me in high school?"

Theo froze, his heart slamming against his ribs. When had she realized? How much did she know?

He couldn't deny it. Wouldn't lie to her. Not now. Not ever.

"I don't know," he managed. "When did you realize?"

"My mother told me." Emma's expression was gentle, understanding. "When I told her I was on your plane, she said to be careful that you had a crush on me."

Like he was dangerous. Like his feelings were something to protect herself against. The irony would have been funny if it didn't sting.

"I've had a crush on you since you stood up to Billy Raye and told him you would tell the entire school he cheated on his history exam so he could continue playing football."

The memory was seared into his brain, the metal locker cold against his back, Billy Raye's meaty hand on his chest, the sick certainty that this was it, he was going to get locked inside and no one would let him out until morning. And then Emma's voice, clear and strong and fearless.

"He was about to shove me into a locker, close it, and lock me inside, but you stopped him." Theo's voice roughened with old emotion. "You saved me that day."

Looking back now, with twenty-twenty hindsight and a black belt in Brazilian jiu-jitsu, he almost wanted to return to that school and dare Billy Raye to try it again. See how it turned out when his victim could fight back.

"And I would have," Emma said fiercely. "But that's a long time ago."

"Every boy has a high school crush. You were mine." The confession came easier than he'd expected. "I felt lucky we were such good friends. But there was a time I wanted to kiss you so bad, it almost killed me."

Years of wanting. Years of wondering what if. Years that had led to this moment, this plane, this storm.

Maybe the universe had always been working toward this. Toward them.

"And now you can," Emma said, her eyes bright with something that looked a lot like love. "In fact, shut up and kiss me now."

Theo's heart swelled so large he thought it might crack his ribs. "With pleasure."

He lowered his mouth to hers, and in that kiss was everything, the boy he'd been, the man he'd become, and the future stretching out before them like fresh snow, unmarked and full of infinite possibility.

Outside, the snow continued to fall, blanketing the world in white. And for once, Theo hoped it would never stop.

CHAPTER 11

*H*is lips crushed against hers with a hunger that stole her breath. The kiss was everything, desire, passion, a desperate thirst for life and love, and this moment that was slipping through their fingers like sand. Emma melted into him, her body responding to his touch the way it had from that first shocking moment at the rental car counter.

God, when she'd seen him standing there, she'd nearly walked past without recognizing him. The gangly, awkward boy from high school had transformed into this, this man. Broad shoulders, confident stance, those intelligent eyes that had always seen too much, now combined with a jawline that could cut glass. The transformation had stolen her words, left her stammering like an idiot while he'd smiled that slow, knowing smile.

And now she was in his bed. In his arms. In so deep, she couldn't see the surface anymore.

The thought sent a spike of fear through her chest even as her body arched into his. This time together was drawing to a close. Tomorrow the storm would end. Tomorrow they'd fly to White-fish, and the real world would come crashing back in with all its complications, questions, and doubts.

How would her family react to this new version of Theo? Her mother had warned her—"be careful, that boy always had a crush on you"—as if his feelings were something dangerous. Something to guard against. But maybe her mother had been right to worry, because Emma was falling. Had already fallen. Was plummeting through space with no parachute and no idea where she'd land.

Was she ready to promise her life and her love to this man?

The question terrified her. She'd known him for years, had been his friend when it cost her social capital, had defended him when others mocked him, had genuinely enjoyed his company when dating the popular crowd would have been so much easier. But that had been the old Theo. The boy who'd hidden in the computer lab and coded his way through high school.

This Theo was different. Confident. Successful. Driven in a way that both attracted and worried her.

She'd watched him work these past two days, hunched over his laptop with that intense focus that shut out the entire world. He had ambition and drive, qualities she admired, but was that all he had? Would he give a family his time and energy? Or would she end up like so many wives of successful men, raising children alone while he chased the next big deal, the next project, the next billion?

Their lips finally broke apart, and he stared down at her, his eyes dark with desire and something deeper. Something that made her heart clench.

"I can't get enough of you, Emma."

Warmth flooded through her at the raw honesty in his voice. She reached up and stroked his face, feeling the slight stubble on his jaw, the warmth of his skin.

"Then please," she whispered, her voice husky with need. "Remind me again of how much I love you fucking me."

The crude words felt foreign on her tongue, she'd never been the type to talk dirty, but with Theo, everything felt different. Freer. Like she could be whoever she wanted to be.

He chuckled, the sound rumbling through his chest into hers. "I don't know. There are emails and a new project I'm working on that are calling to me."

Emma's brows shot up, genuine surprise mixing with a flicker of that old fear. "A moment ago, you couldn't get enough of me."

Was this it? Was this the moment when work would win? When she'd see the truth of what life with him would really be like?

A growl resounded from deep in his chest, primal and possessive and utterly reassuring. "Work or you? I'll take you every time. Every second, every minute, every hour, and all day."

Oh. Oh God. That was exactly what she needed to hear. The words wrapped around her heart like a warm blanket, soothing fears she hadn't even fully acknowledged.

But would it always be this way? In the heat of new love, of course, he'd choose her. But what about in five years? Ten? When the mortgage needed paying, the kids needed braces, and some emergency at work demanded his attention? Would he still choose her then?

The doubt whispered through her mind even as her body responded to his touch. No man had ever made her feel this way, cherished and desired and seen in a way that went beyond the physical. She was falling beyond belief for him, tumbling head-first into something that felt too big, too fast, too real.

"Maybe this time will be fast and hard," she whispered, placing her lips along his cheek, breathing in the scent of him, soap and skin and something uniquely Theo. "And the second time will be nice and slow."

She needed him inside her now. Needed the connection, the reassurance, the physical proof that this was real.

"We're doing it twice?" His voice held amusement and heat.

"Oh yes," she said firmly. "It's been at least two hours, and this time will have to last me until after supper."

He chuckled as he nuzzled the curve of her neck and shoulder, his breath warm against her skin. "I've never had sex so much in one day. You're about to wear me out."

"Good," she whispered against his shoulder, only half-joking. "Then you won't look at any other women."

The insecurity surprised her. She'd never been the jealous type, had never felt the need to stake a claim. But with Theo, everything was different. The stakes felt higher. The potential for loss more devastating.

"There is no one but you," he said, and his tongue traced a path along her neck and shoulder that sent shivers cascading through her entire body.

"Oh, honey," she sighed, surrendering to the pleasure as his lips and tongue worked magic on her skin.

He rose and scooted down the bed, spreading her legs with gentle but firm pressure.

"Theo," she squeaked, suddenly shy despite everything they'd already done.

"Emma, no more talking. Just doing," he said.

His lips kissed her navel, his tongue sliding down her belly in a slow, deliberate path that made her toes curl. When he reached her center and his mouth made contact with her most intimate places, a groan tore from her throat. Her hands clutched at the bed covers, fisting the sheets as sensation overwhelmed her.

"Theo."

She should reciprocate. Should take him in her mouth, honor him the way he was honoring her. But he was thinking of her pleasure first. Putting her needs before his own.

Her chest ached with emotion so intense it bordered on pain. Even as teenagers, he'd done things like this, small acts of consideration that she'd dismissed as just Theo being Theo. Carrying her books when her backpack was too heavy. Saving her a seat at lunch when the cafeteria was crowded. Standing between her and Billy Raye's friends when they'd turned their attention to her after she'd defended him.

She'd been too stupid, too blind to see what it meant. To recognize the crush her mother had apparently seen from miles away.

Had any other man ever put her first the way Theo did?

No. The answer was simple and devastating. No one had ever made her feel this cherished, this valued, this utterly adored.

And she didn't want to lose him.

With every second that ticked by, she found herself thinking of forever. Rings and weddings and vows spoken in front of everyone they knew. A house, not a mansion, but a home filled with laughter and chaos and love. Children with Theo's intelligence and her determination.

The images flashed through her mind with startling clarity, as if her subconscious had been building this dream without her permission.

Was this what falling in love felt like? This terrifying certainty? This sense that her life had been in black and white until this moment, and now suddenly everything was in vivid, blazing color?

She wasn't just falling. She'd already landed. She was giving him her heart, wholly and completely, and the vulnerability of it terrified her.

Then he pulled her legs onto his shoulders, and her thoughts scattered.

"Theo," she cried as he kissed the inside of her thigh, his mouth blazing a trail of fire up to the juncture between her legs.

His mouth moved over her with loving attention, caressing her folds, sending tremors racing through her body as he licked with leisurely confidence. His tongue circled her most sensitive spot, bringing her right to the edge of climax before backing off, then building her up again. The cycle repeated until she was shaking with need, her hips moving of their own accord, seeking more.

"You're mine," he said, raising his head to gaze into her eyes.

The possessive declaration should have annoyed her. She was a modern woman, a feminist, nobody's property. But the words sent heat flooding through her instead. Because in that moment, she wanted to be his. Wanted to belong to him the way she wanted him to belong to her.

A whimper escaped her as he continued his sensual assault.

He placed his hand beneath her, lifting and angling her exactly where he wanted her. Then his tongue thrust deep inside her, and she stopped thinking entirely. Her hands clutched at his head, holding him there as sensation built and built and built until the orgasm she'd been fighting crashed over her like a wave.

"Oh," she cried. "Oh, Theo."

Her body shook with the force of her release, pleasure radiating outward from her core to her fingertips and toes. In a daze, she watched him slide his body up hers, all hard muscle and heated skin and barely controlled desire.

They were both breathing heavily, their hearts pounding in sync. She could feel his pulse against her chest, reassuring her that they were both caught in this madness together. That she wasn't alone in the intensity of what they were feeling.

And then he thrust inside her, hard and deep, and she welcomed him with a cry of pleasure.

"Emma, this is what I dreamed of when I was a teenager." His voice was rough, strained with emotion and effort. "You were who I wanted. Every night I dreamed of taking you just like this. Sometimes it was oral sex, and sometimes it was just like this. So perfect between the two of us."

The confession broke something open inside her. All those years. All that longing. She'd been oblivious while he'd suffered through adolescence wanting something he thought he could never have.

"Theo," she whispered, unable to form more words as he moved within her.

Each thrust felt like completion. Like pieces of a puzzle

sliding into place. How could she have never known that this, this connection, this perfect synchronicity, was waiting for them?

With every movement, he seemed to hit every nerve, every sensitive spot, every stroke reaching past her body to touch her heart directly. This was her nerd. Her very handsome, smart, caring man. The man she loved.

The realization crystalized with sudden clarity. She loved him. Not the way she'd loved him as a friend in high school. Not the casual affection of old acquaintances. But deep, soul-shaking, change-your-life love.

This was the man she was ready to promise forever to. The man she wanted babies with. The man she wanted to grow old with, sitting on a porch swing watching grandchildren play in the yard.

Clinging to him, she felt another orgasm building. Every breath came faster, more urgent. With every gasp they were in sync, one body, one heart, one soul split between two people and desperate to merge back together.

Gazing into his eyes, she could see he felt the emotions as intensely as she did. Could see the love and wonder and terrified joy reflected back at her.

Tears welled and spilled from her eyes as passion surged through them simultaneously. Like fireworks on the Fourth of July, they both came, their bodies locked together in shared ecstasy. When the tremors finally subsided, he wrapped his arms around her and simply held her.

The tenderness of it nearly undid her. This powerful, successful man holding her like she was something precious. Something to be protected and cherished.

After several minutes, she ran her fingers through her hair, trying to regain her equilibrium. How would she ever be the same after this? How could she go back to her ordinary life when Theo had shown her what extraordinary felt like?

"Are you certain about a second time?" he asked, and she could hear the smile in his voice.

"A second, a third, a fourth. Every day," she whispered, wanting forever with Theo. Wanting to wake up beside him for the rest of her life.

He chuckled, the sound rumbling through his chest. "I may have to eat something to regain my strength."

"That's fair," she said, letting her hands explore his body, tracing the muscles in his back, the curve of his shoulder, the dip of his spine. She loved the feel of his skin, the way his muscles rippled beneath her fingertips, the warmth of him pressed against her.

A thought struck her, and she frowned. "Promise me that if I'm so stupid that I don't know something again, you will point it out to me. I feel like a complete idiot for not knowing you had a crush on me in high school."

How much had they lost because of her blindness? What if he'd worked up the courage to tell her back then? Would they have had years together instead of just days?

He licked his lips before kissing her gently. "We were young. We had college before us. It was better that you didn't know."

The generosity in his forgiveness made her throat tight.

"But now," he continued, his voice dropping to that intimate register that made her toes curl, "I'm so glad you're in my bed and in my life, and I don't want you to leave."

Emma's heart squeezed. With a sigh, she kissed him again, pouring all her confused emotions into it. "Let's go eat so that we can do this again before we have to enter the real world."

As much as she loved Theo, she wasn't ready to face anyone outside of this plane. Wasn't ready for the questions and the judgment and the inevitable complications. They were quickly running out of time, but maybe if they ate quickly, they could steal a few more hours in their snow globe of perfection.

"Agreed," he said. "Can we just fly to another destination and continue what we've started here?"

The suggestion was tempting, so tempting. Just fly away together and forget about responsibilities, families, and real life.

"My mother would be furious. And yours too," she said practically, even as part of her wanted to say yes. Wanted to run away with him and never look back.

"It wouldn't be the first time," he replied, and she couldn't help but giggle.

He was right. Their mothers had spoken often when they'd gotten into trouble as kids. Mrs. Morrison calling Mrs. Blake when Theo and Emma had "borrowed" Mr. Peterson's boat to go fishing. Both mothers descended on them when they'd hacked the school website to change their lunch menus—the time they'd been caught sneaking out to watch the meteor shower at midnight.

So how would their mothers feel now that they were together? And not just together, Emma had a feeling this was permanent. That what had started on a snowed-in plane in Missoula would end with rings and vows and forever.

The thought should terrify her. Instead, it filled her with a warmth that started in her chest and spread through her entire body, chasing away the last of her doubts.

Maybe this was crazy. Maybe it was too fast. Maybe they should slow down and think rationally.

But when had love ever been rational?

"Come on," she said, reluctantly pulling away from him. "Feed me so we can do this all over again. We only have tonight left."

Tonight, and then tomorrow, they'd face the real world together. Whatever came next, she was ready. As long as Theo was beside her, she could face anything.

Even her mother.

CHAPTER 12

*L*ater that evening, Theo leaned back against the couch cushions, Emma tucked perfectly against his side, and tried to memorize every detail of this moment. The weight of her head on his shoulder. The scent of her shampoo mixed with the rich aroma of the beef bourguignon Jenny had prepared. The way Emma's fingers traced lazy patterns on his chest, as if she couldn't quite stop touching him even in these quiet moments.

They'd finished an incredible meal, Jenny had somehow managed to create restaurant-quality food in a plane galley, and now they were on their second glass of wine. Outside the window, snow continued to fall, though less aggressively now. Each flake that drifted past felt like borrowed time.

He knew he should be working. His inbox was probably exploding. The new game launch had issues that needed to be addressed. But for the first time in his adult life, work felt like an intrusion rather than a refuge.

"Tell me about your family," he said, genuinely curious despite having spent countless hours at the Miller house growing up. "You haven't mentioned your sisters much at all."

Emma gave a little chuckle, the kind that held more resignation than humor. "That's because we've been avoiding each other. Nothing much has changed. Amelia is still the golden child. Olivia is a teacher and teaches second grade in Billings."

She paused, swirling her wine. Theo waited, sensing there was more.

"Mom and Dad are getting up there in age, and I think Mom thinks if she brings us all home, we'll once again become a close-knit family. It will be a Walton's Christmas, and instead of John Boy, it will be Amelia they will all celebrate."

Theo heard the stress threading through her voice, the old wounds that apparently hadn't healed despite time and distance. He'd spent so much time at the Miller house growing up that he could picture exactly what she described. Could already see Mrs. Miller fawning over Amelia's accomplishments while Emma and Olivia exchanged knowing glances across the dinner table.

As kids, he and Emma had spent most of their time in the basement area Mr. Miller had finished, a sanctuary away from the family dynamics upstairs. They'd played video games sometimes, sure, but mostly they'd studied and talked about the future. About their dreams. Emma had been planning on medical school back then. He'd wanted to become some kind of computer engineer, though his ambitions had been vague and shapeless compared to now.

He'd built an empire since then. But had Emma achieved her dreams? Or had they been sacrificed to Amelia's perpetual spotlight?

"What would it take for you girls to get along?" he asked carefully.

He'd never had brothers or sisters, had spent his childhood in a quiet house with parents who worked long hours and a computer that became his best friend. He'd always been envious of the Miller girls and their noisy, chaotic family. The shouting matches that somehow ended in laughter. The way they could be at each other's throats one minute and defending each other fiercely the next.

Sure, he loved his parents. But he would have killed for a brother or even a sister. Someone to share the burden of being the only child, the only focus of all parental expectations and disappointments.

"That's a question I've asked myself for years." Emma's voice went quiet, vulnerable. "Olivia feels left out because Amelia and I are twins. She's always had a chip on her shoulder and thought we got all the attention. When in reality it was Amelia. Always Amelia. Everything is about Amelia."

Theo had always liked Olivia, the older sister with the sharp wit and kind heart. He could see exactly why she'd feel overlooked. Hell, he'd felt overlooked just visiting their house, and he wasn't even family.

And Amelia? He'd liked her most of the time, except when she was rubbing it in that she'd come in first place and he was second in their graduating class, which somehow made her the smarter one in her estimation.

Uh, no. He'd go against her with an IQ test any day of the week. That valedictorian ranking had been political, not intellectual, and everyone knew it.

"Do your parents realize they pay Amelia so much attention?" he asked, though he already knew the answer.

"No," Emma said with a sigh. "I think my twin demands their attention. This Christmas I'm going to try something new. I'm going to leave the room when it becomes all about her."

Theo chuckled despite himself. Still the same dynamics at play at the Miller house after all these years. The girls couldn't get along, trapped in roles they'd been assigned as children and never quite escaped.

It was a shame they didn't have a brother. Maybe that would have diffused some of the competitive energy.

Emma shifted against him, her voice dropping even lower. "I

love my twin. But do you know what it's like to compete with a girl who always comes in first? Just once, I'd like to be first and for her to come in second. Just once, I'd like to be the twin who is noticed instead of her. Just once, I'd like for my parents to be in awe of my education."

The pain in her voice made Theo's chest ache. He tightened his arm around her, wishing he could absorb some of that old hurt. Somehow, he needed her to understand that Amelia was her sister and, no matter what, she was lucky to have her. That family, even a complicated, messy family, was precious.

But he also understood her frustration in a way few others could. He'd been second to Amelia too. Had felt that sting.

"You know I think she would have come in second graduating high school," Emma continued, her voice taking on an edge. "But one of her teachers gave her just the right number of points to beat you by one. Once again, she was the favored one."

Theo wasn't surprised. While most teachers liked the nerdy kids who actually cared about learning, there were some who wanted the more popular, charismatic kids to win. The ones who looked good in the yearbook photos and gave inspiring graduation speeches.

But for him, it hadn't mattered in the end. Getting the full scholarship to Yale was what mattered, and he'd done that on his own merit. No amount of teacher favoritism could change the fact that he'd built a multi-billion dollar company before he turned thirty.

Success, he'd learned, was the best revenge.

"It's fine," he said, meaning it. "She could have had first and second, though my parents were so proud of me."

"To me it did," Emma said fiercely. "I wanted you to come in first."

Warmth flooded through him, the kind that started in his chest and radiated outward until his fingertips tingled with it.

She'd wanted him to win. Had been on his side even then, when he hadn't known enough to appreciate what that meant.

He took her hand, threading their fingers together. "All that is in the past. My life is pretty damn good right now. Amelia can always come in first as long as you're by my side."

Emma shook her head, but she was smiling as she lifted her wine glass to his. "That's sweet, but just once I'd like to win."

"You'll always be first to me," he said, leaning down and kissing her softly. The words felt like a vow. Like a promise he intended to spend the rest of his life keeping.

An idea struck him, mischievous and perfect. "Let's surprise your parents. We'll have the first grandbaby."

Emma's eyes narrowed and she laughed, that genuine, unguarded laugh he was quickly becoming addicted to. "I think that will be Olivia. Mom said she's bringing home a man for them to meet."

"But I'll be coming home with you," Theo countered, warming to the idea. "If you want to, we can tell them you're pregnant."

She laughed and shook her head. "No, I'm not going to lie to my family. I'm just happy you're going to come home with me. This feels so right."

It did feel right. Felt like puzzle pieces clicking into place after years of being scattered across the table.

Emma shifted, turning to look at him more fully. "How are your parents?"

Theo felt his chest tighten with a complicated mix of love and guilt. "They're getting older. My father works for me now. This way, I know he's not working sixty hours a week trying to keep up at his old job."

He'd hired his father as soon as he'd had the capital to do so, had created a position specifically for him. Not charity, exactly, but close. His father was sharp as ever, but the tech industry moved fast and left older workers behind without mercy.

"But they're both solid gray now. Where did the time go?"

His parents would be disappointed if he didn't come home for Christmas. Hurt, even though they'd never say it outright. They'd raised him to be independent, to chase his dreams, but he knew they missed him. Missed the boy who'd lived in their basement, coding away on projects they didn't understand but supported anyway.

He had to spend time with them. But he hoped to be at both places if the snow ever stopped and the planes started flying again. Hoped to split his time between his family and Emma's, because increasingly he couldn't imagine those as separate things.

Emma's family would be his family soon. If she said yes. When she said yes.

It dawned on him suddenly that the plane no longer shook like a bad roller coaster. The constant buffeting that had become white noise over the past few days had ceased.

"Listen," he said, sitting up straighter. "Do you hear the wind howling?"

They both jumped up and ran to the window like excited children on Christmas morning.

"No," Emma breathed. "I think it's stopped."

Theo pressed his face close to the glass, his breath fogging it slightly. Then he laughed, a sound of pure joy mixed with something that might have been disappointment. "Look, I see a star."

"Star of Bethlehem," Emma said, laughing with him.

"No, it's probably the north star, but it reminds me of the story of Christ's birth."

He stepped up behind her and wrapped his arms around her waist, pulling her back against his chest as they gazed out at the stars beginning to emerge from behind the thinning clouds. The storm was ending. Their time in this snow globe was running out.

"Do you know how much I've enjoyed being with you?" Emma's voice was soft, reflective.

"I've enjoyed it as well," he said, meaning it with every fiber of his being. He couldn't have planned this any better if he'd tried. Getting snowed in with Emma felt like the universe finally giving him what he'd been waiting for since he was sixteen years old.

They were so lucky to have found one another again. So damn lucky.

Emma turned in his arms, and he saw his own complicated emotions reflected in her eyes, joy and sadness tangled together. "Our time together is about to end."

Theo nodded, his throat tight. Then he took her hand and pulled her back to the couch, refusing to let melancholy ruin their last evening.

"What do you want to do now?" he asked.

She chuckled, that warm sound he wanted to wake up to for the rest of his life. "I want you to hold me. Let's drink wine, and then I want you to show me your game that made you a successful business owner."

A spiral of fear trickled down his spine like ice water.

No. Not that game. Not yet.

He wasn't ready to show her that game maybe after he'd asked her to marry him. Maybe after they were married. Maybe after they'd been together long enough that she'd forgive him for creating something so personal, so invasive.

But at this moment, he didn't want her to see it. Because if she did, if she realized what he'd built and why, they might be over before they'd really begun.

"I'm always working on a game," he said carefully, deflecting. "I'd like to drink wine, watch a Christmas movie, and even eat some cookies."

"How old are you?" Emma teased.

"I'm ten," he said, relieved she was playing along.

"If you're ten, then you'll want to play video games," she replied with a grin.

Damn. She had him there.

That was true, but he absolutely didn't want to show her his game. If he could get away with never showing her, he would. But that wasn't possible. Sooner or later, she would know. Would discover what he'd created and the inspiration behind it.

Would she understand? Or would she see it as the obsession it had been?

Just then, a knock on the door saved him from having to answer. The door that separated the cabin from the crew area.

"Come in," Theo called, pathetically grateful for the interruption.

"Sir," Frank said, stepping into the room with his pilot's cap in his hands. "The airport tower said the weather is improving. Tomorrow morning, they'll begin to clear the runways. It will take most of the day. After that, commercial flights will be allowed to leave first. They're expecting us to depart around four p.m."

It was over. Their bubble was about to burst.

Theo forced his voice to remain steady and professional. "Thanks, Frank. Are we all fueled up and ready to go?"

"No, but we'll take care of that first thing in the morning at daylight."

"Good, thanks for letting me know."

Frank nodded and disappeared back through the door, leaving them alone again.

Theo turned toward Emma and smiled, trying to focus on the positive. On what came next instead of what they were losing. "We're going home to Whitefish."

"Yes," Emma said, leaning against his shoulder. "I know I should be excited, but I've enjoyed myself so much being with you. You've turned an unpleasant time into something magical."

Oh, she had no idea what these three days had meant for him. What she'd given him simply by being here, by giving them a chance, by falling with him instead of running away.

"So, you'll fly home with me tomorrow," he said, already planning. "We'll go to my parents' house first and say hello, and then I'll take you to your home."

And while he was there, he would ask to speak to her father alone. Would request permission the old-fashioned way, because Emma deserved that respect. Deserved everything done properly.

Hopefully, the ring he'd commissioned would arrive before Christmas. If not, he would just use the one he and Jenny had created, the one currently sitting in his luggage, waiting for the perfect moment.

Standing, Theo finished off his wine and set the glass down with more force than necessary. Then he helped Emma to her feet and pulled her close, beginning to sway in the confined space.

"What are you doing?" Emma asked, laughing.

"I'm dancing with you," he said, leading her toward the hallway. One slow step at a time. "All the way to the bedroom."

She giggled, and the sound of her happiness filled him with such intense warmth that his eyes actually stung.

Maybe the goofy teenage smart boy really would end up with the beautiful girl after all.

Maybe dreams really did come true, even for nerds who'd spent high school in computer labs instead of at football games.

Maybe, just maybe, everything he'd been working toward his entire life had been leading to this moment. To her.

Tomorrow they'd face the real world. Tomorrow, he'd ask her father for permission and get down on one knee and offer her everything he had.

But tonight—tonight was still theirs.

CHAPTER 13

The next morning, Emma awoke to the pale gray light filtering through the plane window, and her first thought was: *I'm not ready.*

Not ready for their time to end. Not ready to leave the safety of this cocoon they'd built together over three snow-bound days. Not ready to face the stress waiting for her at home, the competitive undercurrent that ran through every Miller family gathering like an electrical wire humming just beneath the surface.

She loved her family. She did. But time with them was often like being on a trampoline, constantly bouncing between trying to prove herself and trying not to care, while Amelia effortlessly landed every flip, and their parents applauded from the sidelines. Someday, she hoped it would all stop. Hoped they could just be sisters without the constant scorekeeping.

But these three days with Theo had been different. Perfect, even. He'd captured her heart so completely that she couldn't remember what it felt like before, that hollow space she hadn't even known existed until he'd filled it.

Maybe she had always loved him. Maybe that's why no other relationship had ever worked, why every boyfriend had felt like settling, like wearing shoes that were almost the right size but pinched in all the wrong places.

After this time together, she didn't want them to ever be apart. She loved this goofy boy she'd been best friends with in school. How she'd overlooked him as boyfriend material, she didn't know, willful blindness, maybe, or just the stupidity of youth. But now she wanted more than friendship. She wanted it all with Theo. The house, the kids, the whole messy, complicated, beautiful life.

With a sigh, she glanced across the pillow at him. He was sprawled out on his stomach, one arm flung above his head, hair falling across his forehead. She had the most insistent urge to reach over and brush it away, to trace the line of his jaw, to wake him with kisses.

But that would be selfish. Today would be exhausting, and he needed his rest after the night they'd shared, a night that had left her muscles pleasantly sore and her heart dangerously full.

Instead, she slipped out of bed as quietly as possible and padded to the bathroom. The shower was a luxury she'd come to appreciate over their stranded days, hot water and good pressure, even on a plane. Tonight she'd sleep in her childhood bed, staring at glow-in-the-dark stars she'd stuck on the ceiling when she was twelve. In that bed, she'd dreamed of finishing school, meeting her husband, having a big wedding with all the fairy-tale trimmings.

And now, impossibly, those dreams might actually come true.

The water sluiced over her as she thought about Theo's journey. How that skinny, bullied kid had created a video game that sold so many units it made him unbelievably rich. She was genuinely happy for him, proud, even. She'd always known he was brilliant, but watching him work these past few days had shown her the depth of his ambition and drive.

She wanted him to know she didn't love him for his money. That she'd have fallen for him just as hard if he were still coding in his parents' basement, eating ramen, and dreaming of his big break. She loved him for the man he'd become and the boy he'd been. And she hoped their friendship would always remain the foundation of whatever they built together.

Getting out of the shower, Emma dried off and dressed quickly, her mind circling back to last night. Why had he been so reluctant to show her his game? He'd deflected, changed the subject, acted like he just wanted to spend time with her. But she'd sensed something underneath, a nervousness, almost a fear.

Was it violent? Did it contain nudity or something he didn't want her to see? What could possibly make him so evasive about the game that had made his fortune?

Or, and this thought sent a chill through her, was it just her? Did he think she wouldn't understand? That she'd judge him for whatever he'd created?

With a sigh, she opened the bathroom door and found him awake, propped up on one elbow, watching her with those intelligent eyes that seemed to see straight through her.

"Good morning," he said, his voice rough with sleep. "What time is it?"

"Almost eight," she replied, trying to ignore how good he looked, rumpled and half-awake. "I'm going to get some coffee. Do you want me to bring you a cup?"

"Yes," he said, throwing the covers back.

The man was completely naked, morning arousal on full display, and damn if her body didn't respond immediately despite having just showered.

"Were you dreaming about me?" she asked, unable to stop the smile.

He grinned, that boyish, unguarded grin that made her heart flip. "Always. Do you want to take advantage of me? I love it when you do. Tie me up, make me your bitch. I'll be yours regardless."

She laughed, genuinely delighted by his playfulness. Thirty

minutes ago, she would have climbed right back into that bed. But now a different kind of curiosity had taken hold.

"Too late," she said. "I just got out of the shower. Besides, I don't want to make you my bitch. I like you just the way you are."

"Hmm, you're nice and clean and smell so good..." He wrapped his arms around her and pulled her into a kiss that sent shivers racing up her spine.

How could he reduce her to a puddle with just a touch? It wasn't fair.

A knock interrupted them. "Sir, the captain wanted me to let you know that we're about to receive fuel," Jenny called through the door.

"Thank you," Theo replied, pulling back with apparent reluctance. "What that means is they don't want us to create any sparks of any kind. So I guess we'll not be making love."

He was teasing, but Emma's practical side kicked in. Probably best to avoid activities that might generate static electricity while jet fuel was being pumped into the tanks.

She reached up and kissed him softly. "Last night will just have to suffice until we get time alone again."

"Yes," he sighed dramatically. "I think I'll jump in the shower real quick."

"I'll bring you some coffee," she said.

If this was what their life would be like every day, this easy domesticity mixed with passion, she was all in. Just as soon as she finished school, she wanted to marry him. All she was waiting for was for him to ask.

And given the way he looked at her, the way he talked about the future, she was pretty sure he would. Maybe even this Christmas.

Emma hurried into the main cabin, where Jenny appeared immediately with a steaming cup of coffee, as if summoned by telepathy.

"Thank you," Emma said gratefully. "Could you get me another cup? I'll take this one to Theo."

"Of course," Jenny replied with a knowing smile.

Emma delivered the coffee to the bathroom, catching a glimpse of Theo's silhouette through the frosted shower door before retreating. This would be a good time to satisfy her curiosity about his game. To understand what people thought of it, to see if it was violent or sexual, or contained something that might explain his reluctance.

But she knew Theo. He'd never been into gratuitous violence. And as far as she knew, he'd never been interested in pornography or anything exploitative.

So what was he hiding?

Back in the main cabin, she pulled out her laptop and settled onto the couch. Jenny returned with her coffee.

"Thank you," Emma said. "You're amazing, you know that?"

"I'll fix breakfast so we'll be ready to go as soon as the tower gives us the all-clear," Jenny said.

"If I were rich, I'd lure you away from Theo," Emma joked. "You're a fabulous cook."

Jenny smiled warmly. "Thank you. I think the crew is ready to go, we can all get home to be with family for Christmas."

"I'm sure," Emma nodded. "This has been quite the storm."

"Yes, ma'am," Jenny agreed, disappearing into the galley.

Emma opened her laptop and navigated to Theo's company website. The homepage was sleek and professional, featuring advertisements for all his games, puzzle games, strategy games, adventure games. But she was looking for the first one, the game that had started it all.

She found it quickly: "Stand Up: A Survivor's Guide."

The reviews were glowing. Players raved about how much fun it was, how engaging the gameplay was, and how it taught valuable life skills. One comment caught her eye: "This game literally taught my son how to handle the bullies at school. Thank you for creating something that entertains, and empowers."

Another: "Finally, a game that addresses the real struggles kids face without glorifying violence."

Bullies? Emma's curiosity intensified. She clicked deeper, reading descriptions and reviews. The game taught middle school and high school students different strategies for dealing with kids who picked on them. There were multiple levels, each one teaching a new approach, verbal de-escalation, documenting incidents, knowing when to get help from adults, and building confidence.

The ad emphasized that it did not condone violence of any kind. Instead, it taught smart, strategic responses that protected the victim while minimizing risk.

Emma found a link for a playable demo and clicked it.

The loading screen appeared, and then—

Her breath caught.

There she was.

Not her actual name. Not a photograph. But the character was unmistakably modeled after her. Red hair pulled back in a ponytail. Blue eyes that flashed with determination. The same stubborn set to the jaw that Emma saw every time she looked in the mirror.

"Come on," the character said, her voice strong and confident. "Let's show them how we don't put up with their crap."

Emma's hands shook as she clicked through the demo. In the first scenario, a bully approached a smaller kid near the lockers and began the familiar taunts—"nerd," "loser," the creative insults that cut deeper than they should.

The Emma-character stepped between them. "Don't make me challenge you. You really don't want me to go to the principal and tell him how you cheated on your exam. And you definitely don't want to hit a girl."

The bully backed off, but shook his fist at the kid he'd been targeting as he walked away.

Emma's heart pounded. She remembered that day. Remembered standing between Billy Raye and some freshman whose name she'd never learned, remembered the way Billy's face had gone red with impotent rage.

The next level loaded. The Emma-character walked down a school hallway when a bully slammed a kid into a locker, shut it, and turned the lock.

Oh my God. Emma's vision tunneled. That had happened to Theo. She'd been the one to make Billy Raye open that locker, to free Theo from the cramped, dark space where he'd been hyper-ventilating.

In the game, the character grabbed the bully by the arm, the animation showed surprising strength, and shoved him to the ground. Then she pulled out her phone and took a picture. Started recording video.

"Mr. Football jock just locked a kid in his locker," the character announced clearly. "So I'm going to post this to social media and show the football team how a girl had to defend someone from getting hurt. Unless you get up right now and open that locker."

By the time Emma finished the demo, she was shaking. She sat there staring out the window at the snow plows working the tarmac, her mind racing through a dozen different emotions at once.

Anger. Violation. Confusion. A twisted sort of pride. Hurt.

This was clearly her image. He'd used actual events from their shared history, moments that had been traumatic for him and, in retrospect, defining for her. It was brilliant, honestly. A game that taught vulnerable kids how to fight back without violence, how to use their voices and their phones and their knowledge of social dynamics to protect themselves.

But he'd never asked her. Never mentioned it. Never allowed

her to consent to having her likeness, her actions, her voice immortalized in a game that had sold millions of copies.

It felt weird. Invasive. Almost stalkerish, if she was being honest.

Now she understood why he hadn't wanted to show her the game. Why he'd deflected last night, changed the subject, tried to distract her with wine and Christmas movies.

Did he think she wanted money? Was that why he'd hidden it? The thought sent a fresh wave of hurt through her chest. After everything they'd shared, after the intimacy and vulnerability of the past three days, did he really think she'd demand payment for her image?

Or was it worse than that? Did he know, on some level, that what he'd done was wrong? That creating this without her permission crossed a line?

The bedroom door opened and Theo walked in, freshly showered and dressed. His eyes immediately found her laptop screen. She watched his face go pale as he realized what she was looking at.

Emma glanced up at him, unable to keep the hurt from her voice. "When were you going to tell me?"

He rubbed his hand across his face, a gesture she was learning meant he was stressed, trying to buy time to think. The fact that he clearly knew she'd be upset made this whole situation so much worse.

"Emma, you were the one who was there for me," he said, his words tumbling out in a rush. "There was no one else I could have used in that game, and I didn't expect it to sell millions. It was something I did in my spare time to keep from going crazy."

Maybe so. But that wasn't the point, was it?

"When were you going to tell me?" she repeated, her voice harder now.

He sighed, looking utterly defeated. "I don't know. I didn't want you to be upset with me. I never expected to sell millions of copies."

"Did you think I would expect money from you? Is that why you didn't want to tell me?"

The words tasted bitter. She licked her lips as rage, hot and righteous, flooded through her. "You're afraid someone is going to get your riches and yet you used my image for your damn game."

"You're right, I should pay you," he said quickly. Too quickly.

"No!" The word came out sharper than she'd intended. "I don't want your damn money. I just wanted you to be honest with me. I just wanted you to tell me what you'd done. Since you didn't tell me, it feels creepy. Weird."

He walked toward her, hands outstretched in supplication. "Emma, I'm sorry. It all started out just as an experiment. Something for me to do while I was at college, and then it blew up so quickly. Once I put it online, it sold so many copies, and soon I was forming a corporation. I always meant to tell you, but I just never did, and now it's blowing up in my face."

How could she trust him if he wasn't honest with her? How could she believe in their future when he'd kept something this significant hidden? Why did it feel like everything she'd hoped for, the wedding, the children, the life together, was suddenly being plowed away like the snow outside?

"Emma, it was never done to hurt you." His voice cracked. "All during high school, I had a crush on you, and then in college, you showed up in the game I created. But this game happened because of our relationship in high school. It happened because you were always the one who helped me."

She gazed at him, this strong, secure man who could buy and sell companies on a whim, who'd transformed himself from victim to victor. Anyone who tried to harm him now would suffer the consequences. He didn't need her protection anymore.

If only he hadn't used her image without talking to her first. If only he'd respected her enough to ask.

"I need some time," she said, standing abruptly. The laptop nearly slid off her knees. "This is creepy, and I don't know what to think. I'm going to pack my bag and go to the terminal."

"No, Emma, please, I want you here," he said, desperation bleeding into his voice.

She shook her head, already moving toward the bedroom. Her chest felt tight, her eyes burning with unshed tears. Quickly, she threw everything into her suitcase, her clothes, her toiletries, the life she'd imagined building with him over three perfect days.

Why did she feel so betrayed? If only he'd told her, she could have accepted it. Could have laughed about it, maybe, or felt flattered that he'd immortalized her heroism. But finding out this way, discovering it by accident when he'd clearly been hiding it, felt fundamentally wrong.

And that had her questioning everything. Every word he'd spoken. Every promise implied in his touch.

She needed time to sort through her feelings, to figure out whether this was something they could move past or if it was a symptom of something deeper. Some fundamental lack of respect or honesty that would poison everything else.

It wasn't every day that someone used your image in a video game without permission. It wasn't every day that your lover turned you into a protagonist for millions of people to see, to control, to play.

Emma grabbed her suitcase and headed for the door, not trusting herself to look back at Theo's face. If she saw the hurt there, she might crumble. And right now, she needed to be strong.

She needed to figure out if the man she'd fallen in love with was real, or just another character in a game she hadn't known she was playing.

CHAPTER 14

heo wanted to kick himself. No, he wanted to do worse than that. He wanted to crawl into a hole and die there, alone with his stupidity echoing off the walls.

He sank onto the leather couch in the plane's cabin, his head dropping into his hands as Emma's face, shocked, hurt, betrayed, burned itself into his memory. That look would haunt him for the rest of his life if he couldn't fix this.

How could I have been so stupid?

Everything had been perfect. Better than perfect. After all these years of wondering what might have been, Emma Miller had walked back into his life at that car rental counter, and it was like no time had passed at all. She was still brilliant, still funny, still the only woman who'd ever seen past his awkwardness to the person underneath. The girl who'd protected him when he couldn't protect himself had grown into a woman who made his heart race with just a smile.

And he'd ruined it.

The worst part was that he'd seen this coming. For years, *years*—he'd known he should tell her about the game. About how her face was the face of his company's flagship product.

About how every time someone downloaded Bully Removal, they were downloading a piece of her, a digital Emma teaching kids the same lessons she'd taught him in the hallways of Whitefish High.

In the beginning, he'd convinced himself he was protecting his intellectual property. He was nobody then, just a college kid with an idea and a laptop. What if she told someone? What if the concept leaked before he could get it to market?

Then the game exploded. Millions of downloads. Billions in revenue. And suddenly he was terrified for a different reason. What if she sued him? What if she wanted half of everything he'd built? What if their reunion was tainted by lawyers and money and ugly negotiations?

But even that wasn't the real reason he'd stayed silent.

The real reason was shame.

As the money piled up, as White Gaming Systems became a household name, the weight of his deception grew heavier. How could he tell her now? How could he admit that he'd used her image, her personality, her actual techniques—the ones she'd taught him—without ever asking permission? Without ever acknowledging what she'd meant to him?

With each passing year, the confession became harder, until it seemed impossible.

And then, impossibly, she'd been right there at the counter, arguing with the same rental car agent, and his heart had recognized her before his brain caught up. When she'd agreed to share his plane, when they'd been snowed in together, it felt like the universe giving him a second chance.

A chance he'd just spectacularly blown.

Theo lifted his head and watched through the window as Emma disappeared into the terminal, her shoulders rigid with anger and hurt. Jenny, his flight attendant, stood by the door with a sympathetic expression that somehow made everything worse.

"She didn't even want the money," he said aloud, his voice

rough. "Did you see that? When she figured it out, she didn't ask for a dime. She just wanted to know why I hadn't told her."

Jenny moved closer but didn't speak. Smart woman.

"Honesty," Theo continued, pressing the heels of his hands against his eyes. "That was always her thing. In high school, she'd call out anyone who lied, even her friends. She said trust was the only currency that mattered." He laughed bitterly. "And I betrayed her trust for what? Because I was scared? Because I was a coward?"

The plane felt suffocatingly empty without her. For three days, they'd been in this luxurious bubble together, talking, laughing, remembering who they'd been and discovering who they'd become. He'd shown her his design process, watched her eyes light up when she understood the elegance of his code.

They'd even kissed. Made love. Gotten closer than he could ever have imagined.

God, that kiss. Soft and sweet and full of promise. The kiss he'd dreamed about since he was fifteen years old, when Emma Miller had shoved Derek Thompson against a locker and told him if he ever stole Theo's homework again, she'd make sure the principal knew exactly who'd hacked the attendance system.

Theo had fallen in love with her in that moment, watching this five-foot-four girl face down a linebacker without an ounce of fear.

And he'd loved her every day since.

He pushed off the couch and paced to the window, scanning the terminal building. She was in there somewhere, probably looking for the nearest gate, the nearest escape route. Away from him.

No.

The word formed in his chest like a fist clenching around his heart.

No, I'm not losing her. Not like this. Not without a fight.

Emma had taught him how to fight, not with fists, but with

intelligence. With strategy. With words that mattered and actions that backed them up.

It was time to use those lessons.

Theo spun toward the crew quarters. "What time is her flight?"

Jenny blinked. "What?"

"Emma's flight. United to Whitefish. What time does it leave?" He was already moving, his mind racing through possibilities, probabilities, ways to make this right.

The pilot emerged from the cockpit, startled by Theo's sudden intensity. "Sir, I can check with the tower—"

"Do it. Please. Now."

While the pilot made the call, Theo's thoughts crystallized into a plan. It was crazy. It was public. It was exactly the kind of grand gesture he'd always rolled his eyes at in movies.

It was also his only shot.

The pilot returned, reading from a small notepad. "United 2847 to Whitefish departs at 3:00 PM. We're scheduled to leave at 4:00."

Theo checked his watch. 1:30. He had ninety minutes.

His heart hammered as the idea took full shape. "Can you get me access to the control tower?"

"The tower?" The pilot's eyebrows shot up. "Sir, that's highly restricted—"

"I know. But I need to make a public announcement. Over the airport intercom system." Theo ran a hand through his hair, aware of how insane this sounded. "I'll donate a million dollars to their expansion fund. I know they're trying to build a new tower, I read about it in the business section last month. They need funding. I need five minutes on their PA system."

The pilot and Jenny exchanged glances.

"Mr. White," Jenny said carefully, "what exactly are you planning?"

"I'm planning to tell the truth." Theo's voice steadied. "I'm planning to do what I should have done years ago. Put my heart on the line. No secrets. No holding back. Just... honesty."

Jenny's expression softened. "And if she still says no?"

The question hit him like a punch to the gut, but Theo forced himself to face it. "Then at least she'll know. She'll know that she wasn't just some image I used. She'll know that she's been the most important person in my life since we were kids. She'll know that I love her." His voice cracked on the last word. "Even if she never forgives me, she deserves to know that."

Jenny nodded slowly, then smiled. "What do you need from me?"

"Help me write this. Please." Theo grabbed his laptop from the side table. "You're a woman. You know what she needs to hear. I need to make this perfect."

For the next forty-five minutes, Theo poured his heart onto the screen. He wrote about high school, about the lockers and the bullies and the girl who'd been braver than anyone he'd ever known. He wrote about college loneliness and the game he'd created to feel close to her again. He wrote about seeing her at the rental counter and feeling fifteen again, helpless and hopeful and completely in love.

Jenny read over his shoulder, occasionally making suggestions. "More emotion here." "This part feels too corporate, make it personal." "Tell her specifically what you love about her."

When Theo's hands started shaking too badly to type, he realized what this was costing him. He'd spent his entire adult life behind screens, behind code, behind the safety of digital distance. This was the opposite of everything in his nature.

This was vulnerability in its purest form.

"It's good," Jenny said quietly, reading the final version. Her eyes were wet. "Really good, Theo. If someone said this to me, I'd forgive them anything."

"Let's hope Emma feels the same way."

The pilot appeared in the doorway. "The tower gave approval.

They want to review your statement first, but you're cleared to come at 2:00." He grinned. "For the record, I think this is either the most romantic or the most insane thing I've ever been part of."

"Both," Theo said. "Definitely both."

At 1:55, Theo and the pilot crossed the wet tarmac toward the control tower. The cold December air bit through Theo's coat, but he barely felt it. His entire being was focused on the folded paper in his pocket and the words he'd rehearsed a dozen times.

Security clearance took ten minutes. Theo would have stripped naked and run through a car wash if that's what it took. Finally, they led him into the tower itself, a utilitarian room full of screens and serious-faced men in headsets.

The tower supervisor, a gray-haired man named Mitchell, took Theo's statement and read it carefully. When he finished, he looked up with something like respect in his eyes.

"Son, I was bullied in school too. Never had anyone stand up for me the way this Emma stood up for you." He handed the paper back. "I hope like hell this works."

"Me too," Theo whispered.

They positioned him in front of a microphone. Through the tower windows, Theo could see planes taxiing, passengers boarding, life continuing as normal while his entire world balanced on the edge of this moment.

Mitchell held up three fingers. Two. One.

The mic went live.

"Good afternoon, travelers," Theo began, and was surprised when his voice came out steady. "For your holiday enjoyment, I have a story for you. A true story about two nerds who recently discovered they share more than just painful high school memories."

He told the story the way he'd written it, the way it had lived in his heart for fifteen years. The bullies. The protection. The crush that had never faded. The game he'd built as a love letter he was too afraid to send.

His voice cracked when he got to the part about running into her at the rental counter. "All the feelings came rushing back. Not teenage feelings, something deeper. Something that made me realize I'd been half-alive all these years without her."

The controllers had stopped working. Every one of them was listening now.

"I was wrong," Theo continued, his hands gripping the edge of the desk. "Wrong not to tell her about the game. Wrong to let fear keep me from honesty. But I couldn't see anyone else as the hero of that story, because there's never been anyone else. Not for me."

This was it. The moment of truth.

"Emma Miller, I've loved you since I was fifteen years old. I've loved you through college and career, and every empty success that meant nothing because you weren't there to share it. This week showed me what I've known all along, there is no one else. There never will be anyone else."

His voice dropped, became intimate despite the hundreds of people listening. "I want you in my life. I want to wake up next to you every morning. I want to build something real with you, not a game, but a life. I want your laugh to be the last thing I hear before I fall asleep and the first thing I hear when I wake up. I want to grow old with you, Emma. I want everything."

Theo took a shaking breath. "If you want my company, it's yours. If you want me to shut it down and start over, I'll do it. None of it means anything without you. I promise you, I swear on everything I am, no more secrets. Ever. Complete honesty, even when it's hard. Especially when it's hard."

The final words came from somewhere deep in his soul. "Please marry me, Emma. Please let me spend the rest of my life proving that you can trust me. Let me protect you the way you protected me. Let me love you the way you deserve to be loved. Please say yes."

Silence.

Then, somewhere in the terminal below, someone started clapping. The sound spread like wildfire, applause echoing through the airport, through the microphone, through the tower itself.

Mitchell turned off the mic, grinning. "Well, hell. That was something. What a wonderful Christms story."

Theo's legs felt like water. He'd done it. He'd laid everything bare.

Now all he could do was wait for Emma's answer.

And pray that love was enough.

CHAPTER 15

*E*mma sat on the hard plastic chair in the terminal, her carry-on at her feet, her face wet with tears she couldn't stop.

Around her, travelers pretended not to stare while absolutely staring. She didn't blame them. They'd all just heard Theodore White, billionaire tech mogul, creator of White Gaming Systems, declare his love for her over the airport's PA system. They'd heard him bare his soul to hundreds of strangers, admitting his mistakes, his fears, his desperate, all-consuming love.

For her.

Emma Miller. NICU nurse from Whitefish, Montana, currently neck-deep in Physician Assistant school and perpetually exhausted. The girl who'd been too smart and too mouthy and too protective of the underdogs to ever be popular in high school.

And Theo loved her.

Had loved her since they were fifteen.

A fresh wave of tears spilled down her cheeks and she didn't bother wiping them away. Her hands were shaking too badly anyway.

He created a game based on me.

The thought kept circling through her mind, equal parts flattering and unsettling. When she'd first seen her face on that screen, her teenage face, rendered in stunning digital detail, she'd felt violated. Used. Like he'd taken something private and made it public without permission.

But listening to his voice echo through the terminal, hearing the raw vulnerability as he explained *why*, everything shifted.

He hadn't used her. He'd memorialized her. Immortalized the girl who'd protected him when no one else would. He'd taken the techniques she'd taught him, the psychology, the strategy, the understanding that real power came from intelligence, not violence, and turned them into something that could help millions of kids.

Kids like Theo had been.

Kids like the ones she saw sometimes in the NICU, the older siblings who came to visit new babies, the ones with hunched shoulders and wary eyes who reminded her so much of teenage Theo that her heart ached.

Oh God, what have I done?

Emma pressed her palms against her eyes, but the tears kept coming. She'd walked away from him. Walked away in anger and hurt pride, too shocked to process what she was feeling. She'd left him standing on that plane looking devastated, and she'd been so focused on her own wounded feelings that she hadn't stopped to think about his.

About how much courage it must have taken for him to build that game in the first place, coding her face pixel by pixel, recreating memories that mattered so much he couldn't let them go.

About how terrified he must have been as the game exploded in popularity, knowing he'd have to tell her eventually but not knowing how.

About how he'd just stood in a control tower and told an

entire airport that he loved her, that he'd always loved her, that there was no one else and never would be.

"Stupid," Emma whispered to herself. "I'm so stupid."

The woman in the seat next to her, a grandmother type with kind eyes, leaned over. "Honey, if that man meant what he said, you've got nothing to feel stupid about. That's the kind of love people spend their whole lives looking for."

Emma turned to her, vision blurred. "He didn't tell me. About the game. About using my image. For years, he didn't tell me."

The woman smiled gently. "And you've never kept a secret because you were scared? Never done something you knew you should do but couldn't work up the courage?"

The words hit Emma somewhere deep. Because yes. Of course she had.

She thought about all the times in the NICU when she'd had to tell parents their baby might not make it, when she'd had to be strong and professional while her heart shattered for them. She thought about the secrets she kept every day, the fear that she wasn't smart enough for PA school, that she'd fail her boards, that she'd chosen the wrong path.

She thought about the conversation with her mother, when Mom had casually mentioned that Theo White had been "completely smitten" with her in high school.

Emma had laughed it off. "Mom, we were just friends. He never said anything."

"Oh, sweetheart," her mother had said with that knowing smile. "Some boys are too scared to say what they feel. Doesn't mean they don't feel it."

It seemed impossible that brilliant, sweet Theo had harbored secret feelings all through high school while she'd been oblivious, treating him like her favorite person to hang out with but never seeing him as anything more.

But now, listening to his voice over the PA system, admitting that he'd loved her since he was fifteen, since the day she'd shoved Derek Thompson against a locker for stealing Theo's homework, it all clicked into place.

All those times he'd looked at her with those soft emerald eyes. All those moments when he'd gone quiet when she talked about other boys. All those years when he'd been her best friend and she'd been too blind to see he wanted to be more.

And then he'd gone to Yale and she'd stayed in Montana, and they'd lost touch, and she'd convinced herself it was just the natural drift of lives going in different directions.

But it wasn't. He'd been nursing a broken heart, missing her so much he'd created an entire game just to feel close to her again.

"People make mistakes," the grandmother continued. "The question is whether the love is real. And honey, what I just heard over that intercom? That was real."

Emma nodded, unable to speak. The woman was right. Everything Theo had said, the way his voice had cracked when he talked about seeing her at the rental counter, the way he'd offered her everything, his company, his future, his whole heart, that wasn't the voice of someone trying to manipulate or use her.

That was the voice of someone who'd been in love for fifteen years and was finally brave enough to say it out loud.

The last three days crashed over her in a wave of memory. Theo in the plane, showing her his designs with that excited gleam in his eyes that reminded her of when they'd studied together in the library. Theo listening with genuine interest as she talked about her NICU babies, about the impossibly tiny humans she fought to save every day, about her dream of becoming a PA so she could do even more. Theo understanding when she pulled out her pharmacology flashcards, quizzing her without making her feel guilty for studying during their time together.

Theo holding her hand during the worst of the storm, his thumb tracing circles on her palm. Theo kissing her for the first time, so gentle and reverent it had made her dizzy.

Theo looking at her like she was the most precious thing in the world.

Those had been the best three days of her life. Better than any vacation, any achievement, any moment she'd experienced in all the years since high school. Because they'd been three days of finally seeing Theo not as the friend she'd lost touch with, but as the man he'd become, successful, yes, but still fundamentally the same sweet, brilliant person who'd made her laugh in the hallways of Whitefish High.

And she'd been falling for him. Hard. Every moment of those three days, she'd been falling, and she hadn't even fully realized it until her mother's words came back to her:

Some boys are too scared to say what they feel.

Theo had finally said it. He'd said it to an entire airport full of people, risking public humiliation and rejection because she was worth the risk.

And she was going to throw that away? Over what? Wounded pride? Shock?

"No," Emma said aloud, startling herself. "No, I'm not doing this."

She shot to her feet, grabbing her rolling suitcase with one hand and swiping at her tears with the other. Around her, people shifted in their seats, watching with undisguised interest. She didn't care. Let them watch. Let them see what happened when love was real and brave and worth fighting for.

In the NICU, Emma had learned that sometimes you only get one chance. One moment to intervene, to save a life, to make the choice that mattered. You didn't hesitate. You didn't second-guess. You acted.

This was her moment to act.

Emma started toward the exit that led to the tarmac, her heart pounding so hard she could feel it in her throat. She had to get to him. Had to tell him that yes, he'd been an idiot for not telling her, but she'd been an idiot too, blind to his feelings, oblivious to what could have been between them years ago. That the last three days proved they were meant to be together. That she loved him, was falling in love with him, had maybe been falling since she saw him at that rental counter, and nothing else mattered.

She was ten feet from the door when it opened.

And there he was.

Theo stood in the doorway, backlit by the gray winter light, his hair disheveled and his eyes red-rimmed. He looked exhausted and terrified and so heartbreakingly hopeful that Emma's breath caught in her chest.

"Emma," he gasped, like her name was a prayer.

Then, before she could say anything, before she could tell him all the words crowding her throat, he moved forward and dropped to one knee right there in the middle of the terminal.

The world stopped.

Emma was vaguely aware of people rising from their seats, of parents shushing children, of phones being raised to capture the moment. But all she could focus on was Theo, kneeling in front of her with her hand clasped in both of his, looking up at her with everything he felt written across his face.

"I meant what I said," he began, his voice rough with emotion. "Every word, Emma. I love you with all my heart. I have since we were kids, and I always will. I don't care about the company, I don't care about the money, none of it means anything without you."

His hands tightened around hers, trembling slightly. "I will do whatever you want. Whatever you need. I'll make the game about someone else. I'll donate every penny it's earned to anti-bullying charities. I'll spend the rest of my life proving that you can trust me, that I'll never keep another secret, that I'll always choose honesty even when it's hard."

Theo's voice dropped, became almost intimate despite their very public audience. "I just want to make you happy, Emma. I want to love you for the rest of my life. I want to wake up next to you every morning and fall asleep with you every night. I want to support you through PA school and celebrate when you pass your boards. I want to hear about your day in the NICU and hold you when it's been a hard one. I want to have terrible arguments and amazing make-ups. I want to build a life with you, a real life, not some fantasy but the messy, beautiful, complicated real thing."

He took a shaking breath. "Please, Emma. Please marry me."

The silence in the terminal was absolute. Even the background noise of the airport seemed to have faded away, leaving just the two of them suspended in this moment. Emma could hear her own heartbeat, could feel the weight of hundreds of eyes, could see the desperate hope in Theo's expression.

She was crying again, but this time they were different tears. Not tears of hurt or confusion, but tears of overwhelming emotion. Of love so big it couldn't be contained. Of certainty so pure it made everything else fall away.

In her training, Emma had learned to trust her instincts. When a baby crashed, when the monitors screamed, when everything went wrong—you trusted your gut. You didn't overthink. You knew.

And she knew this.

She knew Theo. Knew his heart, his kindness, his fierce loyalty. Knew that he'd spent fifteen years loving her from a distance because he'd been too afraid to risk their friendship. Knew that he'd finally found the courage to tell her, and that kind of courage deserved to be met with equal bravery.

This was her person. Her Theo. The boy who'd made her laugh when everyone else made her angry. The man who'd built an empire but still looked at her like she'd hung the moon. The one who'd always been there, even when they were apart, carrying her in his heart.

"Yes," Emma said, her voice breaking. She pulled him to his feet, not caring that her mascara was probably running, not caring that her nose was red from crying. "Yes, Theo. Yes, I'll marry you. Yes, I love you. Yes to everything."

His face transformed, hope blooming into joy so radiant it took her breath away. "You... you mean it?"

"I love you," Emma said, louder this time, wanting him to hear it, to believe it, to know it in his bones. "I love you, and I can't wait to be your wife. I can't wait to spend the rest of my life with you."

Theo pulled her into his arms, and Emma melted into him, her face pressed against his chest, his heartbeat thundering beneath her ear. His arms wrapped around her like he was afraid she might disappear, and she held him just as tightly, anchoring them both in this moment.

Around them, the terminal erupted. Cheers and applause echoed off the walls, people whistling and calling out congratulations. Someone started chanting "Kiss! Kiss! Kiss!" and others joined in, laughing and clapping in rhythm.

But Emma barely heard them. All she could focus on was Theo, the way he was looking at her like she was a miracle, the way his hand was cupping her face so tenderly.

"I'm sorry," he whispered, his voice thick. "Emma, I'm so sorry. I was so afraid I'd lost you. When you walked off that plane, I thought I'd ruined everything. I thought—"

"Shh." Emma pressed her fingers to his lips. "I'm sorry too. I should have stayed. Should have let you explain instead of running away. I was just so shocked to see my face on that game, to realize that you'd built this empire partly based on me, on us. It was overwhelming."

"You had every right to be angry," Theo said. "What I did—"

"What you did," Emma interrupted, "was create something

beautiful. Something that helps kids protect themselves. Kids like you were, Theo." She smiled through her tears.

"I'm sorry you spent all those years thinking I didn't care about you that way. Because Theo, this week, these three days, I've been falling for you. Hard. And hearing you say you've loved me since we were fifteen? That you built this game because you missed me?" She shook her head in wonder. "I'm not angry. I'm... I'm honored. And touched. And so incredibly in love with you that it scares me a little."

Theo's expression softened. "Yeah?"

"Yeah." Emma laughed, the sound watery but genuine. "You turned me into a superhero, Theo. You took that scrappy girl who protected you in high school and made her into someone who could teach kids all over the world how to protect themselves. Do you know how incredible that is?"

"You were always a superhero to me," he said simply.

Fresh tears spilled down Emma's cheeks. "You're going to make me cry forever, aren't you?"

"Only happy tears," Theo promised. He glanced around at their audience, seeming to remember for the first time that they weren't alone. "Though maybe we should continue this somewhere more private?"

"Wait." Emma grabbed his arm before he could lead her away. "I need to say something else."

Theo turned back, concern flickering across his face. "What is it?"

"No more secrets," Emma said firmly. "From either of us. You told me everything today, put your heart out there for everyone to see. I need you to know that I'm all in. Completely. Whatever comes next, PA school stress, long shifts at the hospital, your crazy business schedule, we face it together. Honestly. No holding back."

Understanding lit Theo's eyes. "No more secrets. No more being too scared to say what we feel."

"Exactly," Emma said. "Because I spent fifteen years not knowing you loved me, and I don't want to waste another minute not knowing what you're thinking or feeling."

"Deal," Theo said. "Even when it's hard. Especially when it's hard."

"Especially then," Emma echoed.

"Wait," Theo said suddenly. "I almost forgot. I have something for you."

He reached into his pocket and pulled out what looked like a ring. Emma's heart jumped, until she realized it was made of paper. A printed image of a diamond engagement ring, somehow crafted into a wearable band.

Laughter bubbled up from somewhere deep in her chest, bright and uncontrollable. "Theo, what—"

"The real one is on the way to your parents' house," he said quickly, sliding the paper ring onto her finger with exaggerated seriousness. "I promise. But I didn't want to propose without a ring, so I improvised."

Emma held up her hand, admiring the ridiculous paper creation. It was so perfectly Theo, creative, resourceful, slightly awkward, and completely endearing. This was the same boy who'd once built her a working model of the solar system out of tennis balls and wire hangers for her science project. "It's perfect."

"It's terrible," Theo corrected, grinning. "But it's a placeholder until I can do this properly."

"This is properly," Emma insisted. She pulled him down for a kiss, soft and sweet and full of promise. Around them, the applause started up again, but she didn't care. Let them watch. Let them see what real love looked like, unexpected and imperfect and absolutely worth fighting for.

When they finally pulled apart, both breathing hard, Theo rested his forehead against hers. "Come on. Let's get you home to Whitefish. I need to speak to your father."

"Oh God," Emma groaned. "Dad's going to lose his mind. He's

been trying to set me up with Dr. Morrison from the hospital for years."

"Too bad for Dr. Morrison." Theo took her hand, lacing their fingers together. The paper ring crinkled slightly and Emma smiled. "You ready?"

Emma looked around the terminal one more time. At the families who'd been stranded here for three days, waiting out the blizzard, desperate to get home. They were smiling now, caught up in the romance of the moment, their own frustrations temporarily forgotten.

In the NICU, Emma had learned that sometimes miracles happened. Sometimes the baby who wasn't supposed to make it fought and survived. Sometimes hope won against impossible odds.

This felt like that. Like a miracle she hadn't known she was waiting for.

"Merry Christmas," Emma called out, her heart overflowing. "Merry Christmas, everyone!"

"Merry Christmas!" A little girl's voice responded first, high and sweet.

Then others joined in, a chorus of voices calling out holiday greetings, strangers connected by this shared moment of joy. The weariness of the last few days seemed to lift, replaced by renewed hope. The storm was over. They'd all be home soon. And love, real, brave, beautiful love, had won.

Emma turned to Theo and kissed him again, quick and fierce. "I love you, Theo."

"I'll love you till I close my eyes and take my last breath," he said, his voice solemn. "And even then, I'll go into eternity with your name on my heart."

"That's the most romantic thing anyone's ever said to me."

"Get used to it," Theo said, grinning. "I've got fifteen years of romantic declarations saved up."

They started toward the exit, but before they could reach the door, a woman stepped into their path.

"Excuse me," she said hesitantly. She was in her mid-thirties, with tired eyes and a desperate expression that Emma recognized from the hospital, a parent at the end of her rope. "I'm sorry to bother you, but... what game were you talking about? My son is being bullied at school. He came home last week with a broken nose, and he won't talk to me about it. He won't listen to anything I say. But maybe... maybe he'd play a game?"

Emma's professional instincts kicked in immediately. She'd seen this before, kids who shut down after trauma, who couldn't talk about what hurt them but might respond to indirect approaches. "How old is your son?"

"Twelve. He's in seventh grade."

The worst age, Emma thought. When everything felt like life or death, and kids didn't have the tools to cope.

Theo was already pulling out his phone. "Jenny? Would you have one of the pilots bring in two boxes of those free download coupons?" He paused, listening. "Yes, the ones for the full game. Thanks."

When he hung up, he turned to the woman with a gentle smile that made Emma's heart squeeze. "Ma'am, my team is going to bring coupons for a free download of Bully Removal. It's the full version, usually ninety-nine dollars, but these are completely free. All you have to do is go to our website and enter the code. The game teaches kids strategies for handling bullies without violence. It's helped a lot of kids."

"All I ask," Theo continued, "is that you tell other parents. Tell the school counselor. Tell anyone who might know a child who needs it. We want to help as many kids as possible learn how to protect themselves."

The woman's eyes filled with tears. "Thank you. Thank you so much. You don't know what this means."

"I do, actually," Theo said quietly. "I was that kid. The one with the broken nose and the fear in my stomach every time I walked into school. I know exactly what it means."

The woman impulsively hugged him, then Emma, then hurried back to her family, clutching her phone like a lifeline.

Emma watched her go, then turned to Theo with her heart in her throat. "That's why you made billions, isn't it? Not because you wanted the money, but because you wanted to help."

"I wanted to make sure no kid had to go through what I went through alone," Theo admitted. "If I could give them even a fraction of what you gave me, the tools, the confidence, the knowledge that they could fight back, then it was worth it."

Emma thought about the babies in her NICU, the ones who fought against impossible odds. The ones whose parents sat by their incubators day after day, willing them to survive. She thought about how she fought for those tiny lives, how she poured everything she had into giving them a chance.

Theo was doing the same thing, just for different kids. He was fighting for the bullied ones, the scared ones, the ones like he'd been. Giving them tools to survive, to thrive, to become the people they were meant to be.

She kissed him again, unable to help herself. This man. This brilliant, kind, slightly awkward man who'd loved her for fifteen years and built an empire just to help kids like he'd been.

"Come on," she said, taking his hand. "Let's go home."

They walked out onto the tarmac together, the cold winter air biting but welcome after the recycled warmth of the terminal. Theo's plane waited in the distance, sleek and beautiful against the gray sky.

"Time to get you home to Whitefish," Theo said. "Time to shock both our families when they see us together."

"Time to start our life," Emma corrected. She held up her hand, the paper ring catching the light. "Together."

"Together," Theo agreed, and the smile he gave her was bright enough to outshine the sun.

They walked toward the plane hand in hand, leaving the terminal and its crowds behind. Ahead of them lay Whitefish, their families, Christmas, and the beginning of everything.

Emma thought about her NICU babies, the fighters. The ones who beat the odds.

She and Theo had beaten their own odds. Fifteen years, lost time, fear and secrets and distance—none of it mattered now.

They were finally, blessedly, home.

When they pulled up in front of her childhood home, Emma felt a surge of happiness wash over her like a warm wave. The two-story farmhouse looked exactly as it always had, white clapboard siding, green shutters, the wraparound porch where she'd spent countless summer evenings, but today it seemed different somehow. More welcoming. More like the home she remembered from her childhood, before the sibling rivalry had gotten so intense, before family gatherings had become competitions rather than celebrations.

It was the first time in many years they would all be together, and for the first time in longer than she could remember, she felt genuinely excited about it. She felt happy. Actually, truly happy. She couldn't wait to see her sisters and tell them her good news, to watch their faces when she showed them the ring Theo had fashioned for her on the plane, that beautiful, intricate paper creation that meant more to her than any diamond ever could.

And this year, she was determined that they would put aside their differences and get along. She needed to speak to Olivia privately to make a game plan on how to help Amelia realize she couldn't monopolize all the attention at every family gathering.

Amelia wasn't a child anymore; she was a grown woman, and it was time she learned that the world didn't revolve around her. But Emma felt generous enough today to be patient about it. Maybe even kind.

First, though, Theo wanted to speak to her father. The traditional way. The old-fashioned way. Emma found it endearing, even though she knew her father would probably be shocked speechless. Gerald Miller wasn't the type to expect his daughters' boyfriends, or in this case, her best friend, to ask for his blessing. But Theo insisted, and that made her love him even more.

She waited in the car, watching through the windshield as her parents stood on the porch, her mother bundled in her red cardigan, her father in his familiar flannel shirt. They looked older than she remembered, more gray in their hair, more lines around their eyes. But they looked happy to see her, genuinely happy, and that made her chest tighten with emotion.

Theo came around to open her door, always the gentleman, and then she practically leaped out of the Lexus and ran toward her mother and father, her boots crunching through the snow that had been shoveled into neat piles on either side of the walkway.

"Emma," her mother said, opening her arms wide. "I'm so glad you're here and safe."

"Mom," she said, throwing herself into her mother's embrace. "That was some blizzard, but I'm so happy it happened."

Her mother leaned back, holding Emma at arm's length to study her face. "Dear, I've been worried sick about all of you. I was so afraid that you were either on the roads or stuck somewhere dangerous. I'm just happy you're okay. You have no idea how many scenarios went through my head."

"Oh, Mom, the best thing happened," Emma said, unable to keep the grin off her face. She felt like a teenager again, bursting to share a secret.

Her mother's eyes narrowed slightly, then shifted past Emma's shoulder. "Dear, is that Theo?"

"Yes, Mother. That's how I got here. Theo flew me home in his private jet. The one I called you from, remember?"

Her mother's face broke into a knowing grin, the kind of smile that said *I told you so* without actually saying the words. "I told you he had a crush on you. Didn't I say that? For years, I've been saying that boy was in love with you."

"You were right," Emma said, grinning back. "But I have an even bigger one on him. I don't know how I didn't see it before, Mom. All those years, and I was so blind."

Theo walked up the steps with that easy confidence she'd always admired, his hand extended toward her mother. "Hello, Mrs. Miller, Mr. Miller, good to see you again. Mr. Miller, could I speak with you in private?"

For a moment, her father looked stunned, his weathered face registering surprise and something else, understanding, perhaps, or maybe just the realization that his little girl had grown up. "Son?"

"Yes, sir. I'd like to talk to you in private," Theo said again, his voice steady and respectful.

Emma could see her father was taken aback, clearly he hadn't expected this, but her mother's grin widened until Emma thought her face might split. Her mother had known. Of course, she had. Mothers always knew these things.

Her father patted Emma on the arm, his rough hand gentle against her coat sleeve. "I'll be right back, sweetheart."

As soon as they disappeared inside, Emma giggled, feeling giddy and young and utterly foolish in the best possible way. "Mom, you're not going to believe what happened."

Her mother watched the door close behind the two men, then turned back to Emma with eyes that sparkled with anticipation. "He finally confessed his feelings about you, didn't he?"

"Yes," Emma responded, her voice catching slightly with emotion. "He asked me to marry him and I said yes." She held out her left hand, showing her mother the paper ring that adorned her finger. "This is temporary, he made it for me on the plane because the real one is being shipped here. But Mom, this one is special. He created it himself, folded it with his own hands."

Her mother pulled her in tightly and hugged her, and Emma felt tears prick her eyes. This was what she'd been missing. This warmth. This unconditional love and support. "I'm so happy for you, darling. I've thought for years that you two were perfect for one another. The way he looked at you, even back in high school. Now it's all coming true. Wow," her mother said, pulling back with sparkling eyes, "two weddings to plan."

"Two?" Emma asked, feeling a small flutter of confusion in her chest. "Who else is getting married?"

"Your sister Olivia is engaged to the nicest young man. They ran to the grocery store to pick up some things I forgot, but they should be back soon. You're going to love him, Emma. So much better than that first guy she was going to bring home, what was his name? Marcus? That awful banker who talked about himself constantly?"

Emma felt a moment of confusion, followed by that old familiar feeling, the one she'd promised herself she wouldn't indulge in anymore. Of course, Olivia beat her to getting engaged. She was never first. Olivia, with her perfect life, perfect choices, and perfect timing, had managed to get engaged before Emma even knew Theo loved her. But even as the thought crossed her mind, Emma pushed it away. Right now, none of that seemed to matter. All that mattered was that she and Theo were engaged. His parents were thrilled, he'd called them from the jet and put her on the phone, and his mother had actually cried with happiness. Now she would deal with her family and whatever craziness came with it.

Hopefully, it wouldn't be too bad this year. Hopefully, she and Olivia could make this Christmas the best ever. They were both engaged to be married. They were both happy. That was something they could share, something that could bring them closer together instead of driving them apart.

"I can't wait to meet her fiancé," Emma said, and she was surprised to realize she meant it. "I'm genuinely happy for Olivia. It's wonderful that we'll both be planning weddings."

"We really like him," her mother said enthusiastically. "And he's a rancher. Such a solid, dependable young man. Works hard, treats Olivia like a queen."

But her man was a billionaire, Emma thought, then immediately felt guilty for the comparison. A game creator who had used her image in his best-selling game, who had loved her from afar for years, who had built an empire while never forgetting the girl he'd known in high school. It would be all right. She wouldn't compete with Olivia. Not this time.

"Mother, why do you want us all to get together this year?" Emma asked, changing the subject before her thoughts could spiral. "What's the big announcement? You and Dad are healthy, right? Nothing's wrong? You're not sick?"

Her mother smiled, but there was something mysterious in her expression. "We're fine, sweetheart. Perfect health, both of us. When everyone arrives, I'll tell you all together, but not until then. It's a secret, and I want everyone here when I share it."

That was strange. Her mother wasn't usually one for dramatic announcements or secrets. Emma felt a small flutter of worry in her stomach. "Who hasn't arrived yet?"

"Amelia isn't here. She's driving from Cheyenne, and last I spoke to her, she was stuck in Missoula."

"That's where I was," Emma automatically replied, feeling a pang of regret. "She could have flown with me and Theo."

But then again, when had Amelia ever told anyone her plans

or where she was going? How was she supposed to know her youngest sister was stuck in the same city? Amelia played her cards close to her chest, always had. It was part of what made her so frustrating to deal with.

"It seems you were all so close to one another and yet you didn't know it," her mother said with a shake of her head. "Like ships passing in the night. Olivia was stranded right outside of Missoula too. Amelia is staying somewhere, I couldn't understand her when she called; the connection was so garbled. It sounded like she said 'paramedic,' but I don't think that was right. Maybe 'paradise'? I'm sure she'll explain when she gets here."

They stood on the porch, looking out at the piles of snow lining the driveway, the winter landscape pristine and beautiful under the gray sky. Emma breathed in the cold air and felt something settle in her chest. Peace, maybe. Or contentment. Whatever it was, she liked it.

Just then, the front door opened, and her father and Theo came out, both of them wearing matching grins.

"Congratulations," her father said, his voice gruff with emotion. He pulled Emma into a bear hug, squeezing her tight. "Your mother always said the two of you would get together, but I just didn't see it. I thought you were just friends. Now I do see it, and I couldn't be happier. I hope you'll have as many good years together as your mother and I have had."

Emma slid into Theo's arms, feeling like she was exactly where she belonged. "I'm so happy, Daddy. Happier than I've ever been."

"Hey, did a box arrive today for me?" Theo asked, looking at Emma's mother.

"Not yet," her mother said. "What is it?"

"A surprise," Theo said, gazing down at Emma with those warm brown eyes she now knew saw her as more than just a friend. "A good surprise."

Emma knew exactly what it was. She had the original paper version of it on her finger right now, a precious reminder of how he'd proposed. Her real engagement ring. And this paper, one she would save forever, would keep it in a special box and someday tell their children about how their father made their mother a ring out of paper on his private jet because he couldn't wait another moment to ask her to marry him.

Glancing up at him, she stretched on her tiptoes and kissed him on the lips, not caring that her parents were watching.

"So when is the date?" her mother asked eagerly. "Have you thought about it yet? Spring would be lovely. Or maybe a fall wedding? October is beautiful here."

"Tomorrow," Theo said without hesitation.

Emma giggled, swatting his arm playfully. "Soon," she amended. "We want it to be soon." And she hoped it would be very soon because she was certain he was the man for her. No doubts at all, no hesitation, no second-guessing. She was ready to marry him as soon as humanly possible.

"That would be Christmas," her mother said, laughing.

"What better Christmas present than to make you my wife," Theo said, pulling Emma closer.

This was why she loved this man. This was why she was so certain, so completely and utterly sure that this was right. "Soon, Theo, soon," she said and kissed him again, longer this time. "We're having a White Christmas."

"Every Christmas for us will be a White Christmas," he said with that crooked smile she now knew was meant just for her.

She giggled at the play on words, the double meaning not lost on her. It was true. Marrying a White, marrying *Theo* White, made every Christmas a White Christmas. And she couldn't wait to spend all of them with him, year after year, building their own traditions and their own family.

As they stood there on the porch, wrapped in each other's arms while snow began to fall gently from the gray sky, Emma realized that this was what coming home really meant. Not the house or the place, but this feeling. This sense of belonging. Of being exactly where you're meant to be with exactly who you're meant to be with.

This was going to be the best Christmas ever. She could feel it.

CHAPTER 17

onight was the last night of the cruise, and Amelia Miller intended to make it count.

The bass thundered through the main lounge, vibrating up through the soles of her heels and into her chest. Colored lights swept across the dance floor in time with the music, painting the crowd in shades of electric blue and magenta. She'd been dancing for hours, and her skin hummed with exertion and champagne and the intoxicating freedom of knowing that, for the first time in two years, she had nothing to prove.

The bar exam was behind her. Passed. The job offer from Morrison & Clarke in Cheyenne was signed and sealed. Monday morning, she would walk into that prestigious law firm as Attorney Amelia Miller, but tonight, tonight she was just a woman who wanted to dance until her feet gave out.

Taylor grabbed her hand and spun her around, both of them laughing, breathless. They'd been friends since their first brutal week of law school, bonded by stress, too much coffee, and the shared determination to make it through. Taylor had kept her sane through the worst of it, and when Amelia's parents had gifted her this cruise as a congratulations present, there had been no question who she'd bring along.

"I need a break," Taylor shouted over the music, fanning herself. "And another drink."

Amelia nodded, following her friend back to their table near the edge of the dance floor. She sank into her chair, grateful for the moment to catch her breath. The DJ transitioned into another song, something with a Latin beat that made her want to get right back up.

That's when she saw him again.

He stood near the bar, and even in the shifting lights, she could see he was watching her. They'd been playing this game all week, stolen glances across the pool deck, lingering looks at dinner, that one moment in the elevator when their eyes had met and held for three floors before the doors opened and the spell broke. She'd wondered each time if he would approach, if she would, but neither of them had made the move.

Until now.

He was cutting through the crowd, headed straight for their table, and Amelia's heart kicked up a rhythm that had nothing to do with dancing. Even in the dim light, she could see the confident set of his shoulders, the easy way he moved. Tall, dark hair that looked like he'd run his hands through it a few times, and those eyes. Even from a distance, she'd noticed those eyes, bright green and impossibly expressive.

He stopped at their table, and up close, he was even more devastating than she'd allowed herself to admit. A white button-down shirt with the sleeves rolled to his forearms, dark jeans that fit him perfectly, and a smile that made something low in her belly tighten with want.

"Would you dance with me?" he asked.

His voice was smooth, with just a hint of gravel that made it interesting. Amelia felt Taylor kick her under the table, a clear message to say yes, you idiot, but she was already nodding, already reaching for his extended hand.

"Of course."

His palm was warm against hers as he led her onto the dance floor. The song shifted, and she recognized the opening bars of a Texas two-step. Before she could worry about keeping up, he pulled her into position, and they were moving.

Oh, he was good. Really good. He led with confidence but not arrogance, spinning her out and reeling her back in with perfect timing. Amelia had taken dance lessons in college, a requirement for some sorority formal she'd long forgotten, but she'd never had a partner who made it feel this effortless, this fun. His hand at the small of her back was firm and sure, guiding her through turns she didn't know she could make.

When he pulled her close for an underarm turn, she caught his scent, something clean and masculine with a hint of cedar and spice. It made her want to lean in closer, to press her face against his neck and breathe him in. The thought sent a flush of heat through her that had nothing to do with the exertion of dancing.

The song ended too soon, and they walked off the floor together, his hand still at her back. The contact felt natural, right, like they'd done this a hundred times before.

"You're an excellent dancer," she said, slightly breathless.

"Thank you." His smile was genuine, pleased. "Can I buy you a drink?"

"Please."

She returned to the table while he headed to the bar. Taylor was nowhere in sight, probably out on the dance floor with the guy she'd been flirting with earlier. Just as well. Amelia wanted this man to herself.

He returned with two drinks, something colorful with a tiny umbrella, and slid into the seat beside her. Close enough that their knees touched under the table, and neither of them moved away.

"You've been watching me all week," Amelia said, deciding to be direct. She was tired of games, of waiting. "I kept expecting you to come over."

He had the grace to look slightly embarrassed, his smile turning sheepish. "I know. I'm attracted to you, obviously, but I had to work up my courage. You're..." He gestured at her, as if that explained everything. "Beautiful doesn't quite cover it."

Amelia felt herself flush with pleasure. She wasn't fishing for compliments, but hearing it said so plainly, so honestly, made her chest warm. "What's your name?"

"Ryan." He picked up her hand from where it rested on the table, his thumb brushing over her knuckles. The simple touch sent sparks up her arm. "And you are?"

"Amelia."

"Amelia," he repeated, like he was testing how it sounded. She liked the way it rolled off his tongue. "Want to dance again?"

She was already standing, pulling him toward the floor. This time, the DJ was playing something slow and sultry, all bass and yearning vocals. Ryan didn't hesitate, he pulled her against him, one hand at her waist, the other finding hers. Amelia let her free hand rest on his shoulder, then slide up to the back of his neck, her fingers brushing the soft hair there.

This close, she could feel the solid warmth of him, the lean muscle beneath his shirt. He smelled even better up close, and when he tucked her tighter against his body, she felt the evidence of his attraction pressing against her hip. The knowledge that he wanted her sent a thrill through her that she hadn't felt in years.

For over two years, she'd done nothing but study. No dating, no distractions, nothing but constitutional law, torts, and civil procedure. She'd promised herself that once the bar exam was behind her, once she had that job offer in hand, she would let herself live again. Tonight felt like the permission she'd been waiting for.

When the song ended, Ryan didn't let her go immediately.

Instead, he leaned down, his lips close to her ear. "Want to get out of here? Maybe walk the deck? It's quieter out there. We could actually talk."

Talk wasn't exactly what Amelia had in mind, but she nodded anyway. "Let me tell my friend."

She found Taylor at their table, and leaned down to whisper in her ear. "I'm going. See you in the morning."

Taylor grabbed her wrist. "Do you have your phone?"

"Yes, Mom," Amelia said with a grin.

"Be careful," Taylor said, glancing at Ryan with approval. "But have fun."

Oh, Amelia intended to.

She took Ryan's hand and let him lead her out of the club. The moment they stepped through the doors, the pounding music faded to a distant thump, replaced by the rush of wind and water. The night air was warm and slightly humid, carrying the salt-sweet smell of the ocean. Above them, stars scattered across the sky like diamonds on black velvet.

They walked toward the bow in comfortable silence, and Amelia found herself hyper-aware of everything, the way their hands fit together, the sound of their footsteps on the deck, the way the ship cut through the dark water below.

"I'm sad tonight's the last night," she said, looking out at the horizon. "I wish you'd come over sooner."

Ryan pulled her closer, turning so they faced each other. The moonlight caught his face, highlighting the sharp line of his jaw, the curve of his lips. "You're the first woman I've been interested in for a long time. It took me a while to work up the nerve."

"Divorced?" Amelia guessed.

"No." He didn't elaborate, and she didn't push. Tonight wasn't about histories or complications. "What about you? Why is someone like you on this cruise without a man?"

"I'm celebrating," she said, surprised by how much she wanted to share with him. "I spent two years doing nothing but studying for the bar exam. I finally passed last month, and I start at a law firm in Cheyenne on Monday. My parents gave me this cruise so I could decompress before real life starts."

"Congratulations." The word was simple, but the warmth in his voice made it feel significant. "That's impressive."

"Thank you." She tilted her head, studying him in the moonlight. "So what about you? Why is a handsome man like you cruising alone?"

"Needed a break from work," he said with a shrug. "Sometimes you have to step away from everything to remember who you are."

Before she could respond, he cupped her face in his hands and kissed her.

The world narrowed to the press of his lips on hers, warm and sure. He started gentle, almost questioning, but when Amelia made a soft sound of approval and opened to him, the kiss deepened. His tongue swept into her mouth, and she gripped his shoulders, suddenly dizzy with want. Heat flooded through her, pooling low in her belly, and she pressed closer, needing more.

When they finally broke apart, both breathing hard, Amelia could only stare at him.

"I haven't been kissed like that in years," she whispered.

Ryan's laugh was low and rough. "I haven't given a kiss like that in years."

Amelia made a decision. Life was short, and opportunities like this didn't come along often. She was tired of being careful, of always doing the responsible thing. Tonight, she wanted to be reckless.

"You're not married, right?" she asked, just to be sure.

"Single," he confirmed. "Very single."

"Good." She ran her hand down his chest, feeling the solid muscle beneath the fabric. "Because I think we should go back to your room."

Ryan's eyes darkened, his pupils blown wide with desire. "You sure?"

"Very sure." Amelia pulled him closer, letting him feel how much she meant it. "We're two single people on the last night of a cruise. Let's not waste it."

A slow smile spread across his face. "My cabin. I have a suite. No roommate."

"Perfect."

They practically ran to the elevators, both of them grinning like teenagers. In the elevator, Ryan backed her against the wall and kissed her again, his hands on her waist, his body pressing her into the cool metal. By the time they reached the Verandah Deck, Amelia was trembling with anticipation.

His suite was nicer than her cabin, a separate bedroom, a small sitting area, and a balcony that overlooked the dark ocean. But Amelia barely registered any of it. The moment Ryan locked the door behind them, the air between them shifted, crackling with tension.

She reached behind herself and slowly unzipped her dress, letting the fabric slide down her body and pool at her feet. She stood before him in just her black lace bra, matching panties, and heels, watching his face as he took her in.

"Damn, Amelia," he breathed, and then he was on her, his hands in her hair, his mouth claiming hers with a hunger that matched her own.

She fumbled with the buttons of his shirt, desperate to feel his skin against hers. When she finally pushed the fabric off his shoulders, she had to pause and appreciate the view. His chest was beautifully defined, all lean muscle and smooth skin that she immediately wanted to explore with her hands, her mouth, everything.

"Tell me you have protection," she said against his lips.

"Multiple condoms," he assured her, his voice rough with desire. "We're covered."

"Thank God." She reached behind her back and unhooked her bra, letting it fall away.

Ryan's gaze dropped to her breasts, and the raw want in his expression made her feel powerful, desired in a way she hadn't in too long. Before she could say anything else, he scooped her up and carried her to the bedroom, laying her down on the bed with surprising gentleness.

"I've been thinking about this all week," he said, his hands running up her thighs.

"Then stop thinking," Amelia said, reaching for him. "And start doing."

He grinned, that devastating smile that had first caught her attention. "Oh no. We're taking our time with this. I want to savor every second."

And he did.

Available Everywhere

A Dear John letter, Amnesia and a Second Chance at Love

When a roadside bomb in Kabul, Afghanistan exploded his Humvee, and wiped his memory of the last ten months, Tyler Ferguson is sent home for Christmas. He can't wait to see his fiancée.

When Kelsey opens her door and the man she'd sent a Dear John letter too is standing on her porch, she fears the worst. Until she realizes he doesn't remember the breakup. Has life given her a second chance with the man she still loves? At least until his memory returns.

Available Everywhere
Also Available in Audio.

Nailing the Billionaire
Nailing the Single Dad
Box Set

Secrets of Mustang Island
Secrets of a Summer Place
Secrets of a Runaway Bride
Secrets From the Past
Secrets of a Reckless Life
Secrets of a Hidden Life
Secrets of a Midnight Letter

Secrets of Mustang Island Novellas
The Summer I Loved You
When We Meet Again
Christmas at Mustang Island

The Langley Legacy
Collin's Challenge

Short Sexy Reads
Racy Reunions Series
Paying For the Past
My Christmas Soldier
Cupid's Revenge

Western Historicals
A Hero's Heart
Second Chance Cowboy
Ethan

American Brides
**Katie: Bride of Virginia

Angel Creek Christmas Brides
**Charity
**Ginger
**Minne
**Cora
Angel Creek Christmas Box Set

Bad Girls of the West
Scandalous Sadie
Ravenous Rose
Tempting Tessa
Nellie's Redemption
Bad Girls Box Set

The Burnett Brides Series
The Rancher Takes A Bride
The Outlaw Takes A Bride
The Marshal Takes A Bride
The Christmas Bride
Boxed Set

Lipstick and Lead Series
Desperate
Deadly
Dangerous
Daring
Determined
Deceived
Defiant
Devious
Lipstick and Lead Box Set Books 1-4
Lipstick and Lead Box Set Books 5-9
Lipstick and Lead Box Set Books 1-9
**Quinlan's Quest

Mail Order Bride Tales
**A Brother's Betrayal
**Pearl
**Ace's Bride

Scandalous Suffragettes of the West
**Abigail
Bella
Mistletoe Scandal

Southern Historical Romance
A Scarlet Bride

The Cuvier Women
Wronged
Betrayed
Beguiled
Boxed Set

The Debutante's of Durango
The Debutante's Scandal
The Debutante's Gamble
The Debutante's Revenge
The Debutante's Santa
Box Set

**** Denotes a sweet book.**

Want to learn about my new releases before anyone else? Sign up for my New Book Alert and receive a complimentary book.

Sylvia McDaniel is a USA Today Bestselling author with over one hundred western historical and contemporary romance novels under her belt. Known for creating memorable bad boys and good girls who can't help getting into trouble, she spends her days weaving compelling tales filled with heart, humor, and unexpected plot twists. Her family-oriented stories have earned her a loyal fanbase, and she's always dreaming up new ways to keep her readers hooked.

Married to her best friend for over thirty years, Sylvia recently relocated to Colorado, where she enjoys hiking and taking in the natural beauty of the forest that borders their home. Their spoiled dachshund, Zeus (who has his own column in her newsletter), and brat dog Bailey keeps them company on their adventures.

Though their grown son still resides in Texas, Sylvia keeps close ties to her southern roots, especially when it comes to football. A dedicated fan of both the Denver Broncos and the Dallas Cowboys, she's happiest when they're winning.

Love books? Love deals? Love a little mischief? Sign up for my
Substack—it's free!
Click Here
The End

www.ingramcontent.com/pod-product-compliance
Lightning Source LLC
Chambersburg PA
CBHW060459300726
48975CB00008B/2571